# She'd tried to put the past behind her

When Professor Jana Fitzgerald's new neighbor turned out to be none other than famous exposé writer Zack Devlin, Jana was terrified.

She'd carved a new life for herself in Illinois, far removed from her Hollywood childhood and the scandalous headlines that had tormented her family. And now this man threatened to destroy her orderly existence.

But Zack Devlin's intentions were far deeper than Jana could have ever imagined....

# After the Stars Fall

## Bethany Campbell

# Harlequin Books

TORONTO • NEW YORK • LONDON
AMSTERDAM • PARIS • SYDNEY • HAMBURG
STOCKHOLM • ATHENS • TOKYO • MILAN

ISBN 0-373-02726-5

Harlequin Romance first edition November 1985

# CHAPTER ONE

FOR A TIME she thought the pain would defeat her, but the magic moment flowered when she could stand it, grew so familiar with it that it became a friend, and then somehow the pain went away, disappeared, and she was running almost without effort. Running became as natural as breathing, and her legs moved like things enchanted. She felt free, complete, invulnerable.

Jana could feel the perspiration dampening the back of her blue Eastern Illinois Panthers T-shirt, feel the sidewalk stinging her feet through the soles of her blue-striped running shoes. The September morning was hot, but other runners were out and the campus was crowded with returning students. A fat man in red jogging shorts was puffing across the campus, wheezing mightily, and Jana winged past him as if she had Mercury's mythic shoes. The fat man was Professor Pomfrit, of the Speech Department, and she gave him a smiling "Hi" as she breezed past. *He must be trying to reduce again,* Jana thought with amusement. From the pained expression on his round red face, he certainly wasn't jogging for the joy of it.

"Show-off!" Professor Pomfrit called after her, and Jana shot him a grin over her shoulder. She was behind Old Main now, the tall administration building that dominated the campus and the town. Unlikely as it was, here in the middle of the Illinois plains, Old Main was a castle, four stories tall and topped with towers that seemed as if they should have bowmen in chain mail atop them, or at the very least, inside the tallest tower, a captive princess. Jana loved the old building, the element of fantasy it gave the campus.

She ran past the flower gardens at the center of the campus, the tall gladioli still blooming like flames in the blue September air. She thought she would cut across to Buzzard Hall, the building where she taught journalism, then head for home and a cold tingling shower.

She raced past the library, which almost matched Old Main in its elegance, with its vaulted windows and soaring medieval lines. Near the tennis courts, she recognized another runner, Ralph Sandler, a professor in the English Department.

"Hey, it's twinkletoes," Ralph said, giving her a slightly pained smile. "I'm out of shape. You, I see, are in peak physical condition. Damn, but you look as if you're enjoying yourself."

"I am!" Jana said, smiling impishly. She fell in beside him easily. Her lightness and speed could keep even distance with his longer, but obviously protesting, legs.

"You're not quite human, you know," Ralph complained grumpily. "Sometimes I don't think there's a human being in there at all. You're some kind of android or something. Nobody could *like* doing this."

"I do!" Jana said pertly. "Cleans out the brain."

"Because you can't think of anything but the pain," Ralph countered. "Ugh! Heard from Les?"

Jana's high lowered itself several notches. "Les is safely ensconced in Cairo, already teaching his students the deep mysteries of American newspaper production, and his only misadventure to date is that a camel spit on him."

"Ha!" grunted Ralph. "Ouch, it hurts to laugh, too."

"You'll get your stride," she said.

"Old Les had better watch out for himself," puffed Ralph. "I hear the J. Department is getting quite a celebrity to fill in for him while he's gone. A real lady-killer. What's his name—Devlin. I hear half the female faculty members are already swooning. I thought Les would have pinned you down with an engagement ring as insurance."

Darn, thought Jana, and the bottom fell out of her lovely runner's euphoria. Ralph had managed to hit two of her sorest spots within the space of two minutes.

"Nope," she said with false brightness. "I'm like Pinocchio. I've got no strings to hold me down. And I'm not about to swoon over Zack Devlin. Especially when he gets to teach the course *I* wanted."

"Aha!" said Ralph, who seemed to be sliding into the feeling of physical ease as swiftly as she was sliding out. "Professional jealousy? Academic envy rears its ugly head."

"Women can have ambitions, too," Jana murmured. She didn't want to talk about it. Even to as nice a guy as Ralph.

"Well, getting Devlin's quite a coup. You can't deny that."

Jana smiled grimly. "A guy with both the Pulitzer Prize and the National Book Award? Let's say it doesn't hurt. But I'm still not impressed. I don't like literary hatchet jobs."

"Hatchet jobs? I thought *Roses for Rama* was supposed to be a masterpiece of reporting. The rise and fall of a cult and a bogus swami in California. Complete with the suicide of a sleazy has-been actor. A searching portrait of social madness and all that good stuff.''

"Not my cup of tea, that's all," Jana said as lightly as she could. "And a cup of tea and a good shower are what I'm ready for, I think. See you around, big guy."

She veered left, cutting across the lawn in front of one of the dorms, giving Ralph a farewell wave she hoped looked cheerful. Her heart was starting to pound in a way that hurt. Ralph couldn't know. He couldn't have known that his banter hurt her as much as if she'd fallen on broken glass. He couldn't know that one of those socially mad people in Rama's cult was her brother. Or that the "sleazy has-been actor" who committed suicide when Rama bilked him out of not only his last dime but his last shred of dignity had been a man that Jana had been fond of once long ago, when she was a child. Ralph didn't know that because he didn't know who Jana was. Or rather, who Jana had been. Not that who she had been was important. Not at all. It was who her father had been. And that was something Ralph never needed to know. Nor anyone else.

Jana was eleven when she learned that being the child of a celebrity was a special kind of hell, a personal hell, because paradoxically it was so public. And her father had been no ordinary celebrity. At first, before his fame became destructive, Jana had enjoyed it all with a child's healthy egotism. Her father, Kevin O'Dwyer, was that handsome blue-eyed Irishman who'd set female American hearts throbbing like overheated engines with his first starring role in Hollywood—as the Trojan hero Aeneas in one of those gaudy historical productions when gaudy historical productions were the rage. With his black Irish, rough-hewn good looks and his wonderful voice, honed to a fine instrument by his

London stage training, he could have merely stared into the camera with those piercing eyes, read from the phone book and made women's knees knock.

Jana and her brother Kevin, Jr., or Jay-Jay and Kevvie, as her father called them, were golden children in a golden time. Their pictures were splashed in papers and fan magazines almost as often as their father's. For Kevin O'Dwyer, in spite of the legions of women who fawned on him, was first and foremost a family man. In that multitude of stories, her father always said he loved his wife, but yes, by the gods, there was another woman, the most beautiful colleen in the world—his black-haired sapphire-eyed daughter, Jay-Jay. Who could not see her and lose his heart forever? And what man could ask for more than a wife such as his own and two such beautiful children? The gods had indeed been good to him.

Jay-Jay had loved him with all her heart. And then the gods played a trick so monstrous it had nearly destroyed them all. Hollywood was filming yet another historical epic, *Guinevere*. Kevin O'Dwyer was cast as Lancelot, the knight so pure that no woman could tempt him. Another British actor of almost unbelievable status was imported for the role of Arthur, and playing Guinevere, the queen who betrayed Arthur and greased Lancelot's descent into hell, was Letitia Farrell.

Tish Farrell. Her platinum-blond hair, her smoky eyes, her flawless figure made her the most sought-after actress in the tinsel wonderland that was Hollywood. Her love life was a series of scandals that the press gloried in. She was the sort of woman who becomes a goddess in her time, a creature of myth. She fell in love with Kevin O'Dwyer, and he fell in love with her. The romance, with all its crazed flamboyance, crowded the national news off the front pages. And Jay-Jay and Kevvie were no longer golden children in a golden time. They were creatures trapped in a circus straight from hell.

Tish Farrell took their father away as easily as someone might lead a poodle away on a leash of leather and rhinestones. They were the couple America loved to hate, yet couldn't get enough of. Before Tish Farrell, Kevin O'Dwyer had been a fine and handsome actor who loved his Hollywood salary and hated his Hollywood pictures—a conflict, he used to joke, he had learned to live with.

But when he married Tish Farrell, he became a genuine example of that mysterious thing the studios most loved: Kevin O'Dwyer became a *star.* The combination of Tish Farrell and her wild Irishman commanded salaries that were impossibly large. But when Kevin O'Dwyer became a star, he destroyed Kevin O'Dwyer the person. And he destroyed much more than that.

He destroyed all the security Jay-Jay had ever known. He destroyed her mother, who had breakdown after breakdown, until at last, one moonless night when Jana was twenty-two, her mother gave up fighting the endless depression and let it take her—to a motel room in Encino and a bottle of sleeping pills. He destroyed Kevvie, who became a heavy drug user by his fifteenth year and who found whatever sanity he could by drifting from commune to commune through California. After the *Rama* episode, he simply drifted away again, and the last she'd heard he was living on brown rice and mantras in Oregon and didn't want to communicate with her, the only surviving member of his family. Kevin O'Dwyer destroyed himself, too, completely and with a vengeance. He was married for six tumultuous and all-too-well publicized years to Tish Farrell. He made a dozen movies that he loathed himself for making. He began to drink. He began to brawl. Then he ended up getting divorced and remarried to another beautiful actress, and then another—so many times that Jana stopped counting—until finally he drank himself to death, having made and wasted a fortune. All that was left was a mortgaged house, an unpaid-for Cadillac, a few paintings, a handful of jewels. Jana got enough from the estate to put her through graduate school, and Kevvie probably gave his share away to whatever guru or holy man he followed at the time.

She had survived, somehow and against all odds. She had survived by the same discipline that made her a good runner—a discipline of iron. She had worked hard, had excelled at school, had excelled in graduate work. She had a job in the Journalism Department at Eastern and was promoted to associate professor at the age of twenty-six. She had taken all the shattered pieces and created a new self.

A healed broken bone is stronger than an unbroken one, she had read. She believed it. All her early sorrow had taught her lessons never taught in classrooms.

The hardest lesson was that people who fell in love were fools. Her mother had been destroyed by her love for Kevin O'Dwyer. Kevin O'Dwyer, in a longer and more complex way, was destroyed by his love for Tish Farrell. She and Kevvie had suffered unspeakably because of this madness people called love. She learned young how much love could hurt.

Not that she was a cold or unaffectionate person. Not that she hated men. The experience hadn't warped her. It had only taught her that romantic love was a form of craziness. She supposed she would marry. She supposed she would be happy. But she would choose someone who was safe, whom she respected and could trust. She might even choose Les. He was bright, he was ambitious, he was unexciting but dependable, and he wanted the same kind of life she did—quiet and filled with meaningful work. That she was not in love with him didn't bother her. It was, in fact, a point in his favor.

Jana was almost home now, within a block of her little Victorian house that sat, almost like a miniature, among the larger Victorians that lined Seventh Street. She slowed her pace and tried to force all thoughts of the past away. Damn Ralph Sandler anyway for making her open up that whole can of worms again. And damn Zack Devlin for helping him to do it—even though the man wasn't here yet. He was the kind of reporter she hated, digging up all the dirt and assembling it in pretty designs, the better for the world to behold. She didn't look forward to having him in the department as Les's temporary replacement, and she certainly wasn't going to be impressed with him no matter how many awards he'd won. She wished he'd go back to wherever he came from and let her teach feature writing. She didn't think of herself as a great writer, but she knew she was a fine teacher. It was a different kind of art, the art of teaching, and she was good at it. Devlin probably wouldn't know a lesson plan from his Smith-Corona.

She realized now how tired she was, and became irritated that the run, instead of scrubbing her brain clean, was only muddying it with thoughts she didn't need to have.

There was a U-haul trailer behind a black Fiat sports car in front of the house next door to hers. New neigh-

bours moving in, she thought. The Babcocks, who lived
in the beautiful high Victorian house, were in Indone-
sia. Like Les, Martin Babcock had a semester's grant to
teach overseas. She ought to be thinking about apply-
ing for one—a grant on a résumé helped advance a
career.

As she drew near her house, she felt a glow of pride.
A funny little house, it looked like something that belonged in a fairy tale, not on this prosperous-looking
street with all its Midwestern mansions. She supposed
it had originally been a guesthouse or a mother-in-law
house. Whatever its past, it was home now, and she felt
as proud of it as if she'd built it herself, stick by stick.
A home. The first place that had felt like home
since...but she didn't want to think about that.

She looked down and saw that her left shoelace was
untied. Too close to home to worry about that now, she
thought.

And at that moment she ran into a brick wall.

Except it wasn't a wall, it was a man, a tall hard man,
and she'd crashed right into him. Something else
crashed to the ground, as she staggered backward, then
felt herself tripping on the loose shoelace.

Strong hands grasped her roughly to keep her from
falling, and she stared in pain and surprise into an angry face. A lock of his carefully barbered black hair
hung over his forehead, probably knocked out of place
by the force of the collision. The eyes glaring at her were
a peculiar shade of hazel—almost yellow, like a cat's,
and his mouth, which curled in contempt under a black
mustache, did not look kind.

"All the people around here run," growled the man.
"It makes me wonder what in hell they're running
*from*."

"I—I'm sorry—" Jana stammered. She must have run into him rather hard, she thought, because she felt distinctly odd, almost sick. The man was holding her tightly by her upper arms, and it seemed as if his fingertips were points of fire against her bare flesh. She was suddenly out of breath and felt strange, as if her stomach had got dizzy, if such a thing were possible.

"Are you all right?" he asked brusquely, the yellow eyes raking her up and down.

"I—I think I knocked a little wind out, that's all," she panted. Suddenly she didn't like that craggy face so close to hers, those hard hands gripping her arms. "I can stand by myself. I'm okay," she said, still panting.

He released his grip and straightened. He was, she saw, quite tall, well over six feet, and his shoulders were broad and square beneath the yellow T-shirt he wore.

"Good," he said, rubbing his hands on his jean-clad thighs. "I don't like holding sweaty women. Unless, of course, the sweat's engendered by the heat of passion."

Jana bristled, her heart still pounding hard. The man was attractive—and knew it. Her least favorite type.

"Sorry," she said, trying to sound calm. "Running's my passion. I hope I didn't hurt you."

"A little thing like you?" He gave a snort of laughter. "No, my dear sweaty little klutz, you didn't hurt me in the slightest. What you have probably destroyed beyond repair is my typewriter."

Jana looked down in horror at the machine lying at their feet. An office-model electric typewriter was lying on its back like an injured turtle. Her hand flew to her mouth in horror. She was so attached to her own typewriter that to see it lying so would be like seeing a favorite dog lying with all four feet pointed heavenward, its soul departed.

"Oh, nooo," she breathed, raising her face and encounter those implacable yellow eyes again. "Oh, good grief! I'm sorry! Truly sorry! I'll pay for the repairs." She saw a cartoon image of her first paycheck flying away on little wings.

"Are you one of the famous Oaf Sisters of Eastern Illinois? How many people have you blundered into today, or am I the first? Is this a demolition derby? Or do you have a quota and call it quits after a certain number?"

Jana felt her face getting hot with anger. She found this man disturbing—disturbing in ways she did not understand. His snide tone was probably justified, but she felt her control skittering away.

"Don't be rude," she said, tossing her head. "I said I'd pay for repairs. It was an accident."

"So was the Ashtabula Train Disaster," the man sneered, putting his fist on a lean hip. "Didn't you hear the keyboard give up the ghost when it hit? We're not talking repairs, lady. We're talking new machine. Not that it can be replaced. I had a sentimental attachment to it. We've been through a lot together, that typewriter and I."

"So sue me for mental anguish," Jana spat, taking a step back from him. His presence was too powerful; it threatened to overwhelm her. She could swear she saw lightning flash in those dark-lashed yellow eyes. "I'll pay for the whole machine, if that's what you want. I may eat canned beans for the next three months, but far be it from me to ruin a little boy's toy and not make it up to him."

"I am not," he said with infinite scorn, "a little boy. And you are not only a public menace, you're a mouthy public menace. I want your name and your address and proof you're who you say you are."

"My name is Jana Fitzgerald," she said, taking another step backward to protect herself from something, though she was not sure what. She had almost said, "MY name is Jay-Jay O'Dwyer." *Damn the past and thinking about the past*. It made one act stupidly in the present and bump into obnoxious men carrying expensive typewriters. Years ago she had taken her mother's maiden name, had lived with it so long it seemed natural, and now, after one bad afternoon bout with past memories and present stresses she had almost reverted.

"And," she continued, "you don't have to get my address. We're neighbours. I am, I'm sorry to say, living next door to you. I'd hoped the Babcocks had rented their home to nice neighbourly folk, but apparently they haven't. So take your poor broken little machine downtown and see what the damage is. Put the figures in my mailbox and I'll make sure that you're reimbursed. By mail. Because I don't want to talk again to a man as unpleasant as you. Ever. In my entire life. Now, if you'll excuse me, I'll go into my house, and you will not have to stare at me any longer with that expression on your face that seems to say I am less than an insect to you. Good afternoon."

She knew she was being ruder than she ought to be, but suddenly all she wanted was the order and safety of her house. Breaking somebody's beloved typewriter was, she knew, a crime that possibly merited punishment by death, but she felt as if she'd come to breaking something far more vital—that barrier between her and her own past.

But the man was blocking her way and unaccountably, although his face was still stern, even pained, there was something like laughter in his eyes.

"It's a spunky little thing, eh?" he said, his lip curled slightly with the hint of a smirk.

Her teeth were clenched. "I just told you to put the bill in my mailbox and that I didn't wish to talk to you any longer. I just said goodbye. If you have difficulty with the English language, I'll say it again. *Goodbye.*"

Still he did not move from her path, so she stepped off the walk and went around him. "I only wish," she said, her teeth still clenched, "that when I hit you, I had been in a car, not on foot."

Her insult didn't have the withering effect she'd hoped for. She heard a hearty laugh behind her, and she straightened her back, knowing she could not, for all her effort, look dignified in a sweaty T-shirt, rumpled running shorts and old shoes, one of which was still untied.

She kept stalking toward her little house.

"By God it *does* have spunk!" he laughed behind her, and she squared her shoulders in fury. In her determination to make an effective exit, she nearly tripped over the loose shoelace again and was rewarded with another whoop of his laughter.

Safely inside her house, she felt her spine go limp, her shoulders sag. She glanced around her living room, and the glow she usually felt was not present.

The little living room looked warm, but not special. The antique furniture she had saved for and bought, piece by piece, seemed attractive, but was only a collection of objects assembled from other people's lives, not her own. The madcap collection of rag dolls that sprawled on the love seat and rocking chairs no longer seemed witty to her, but only a silent assembly of voiceless stuffed things, things without life.

*This is*, she told herself, *no time to go philosophical and critical on yourself. You let it happen again. You let the past come through, and this is the price you pay. You are Jana Fitzgerald, Associate Professor of Journalism. You have come away from the glitz and glitter of Hollywood and a crazy childhood, and you have built yourself a sane and sensible life in the middle of America. You have made yourself a career and you have made yourself a home and you have made yourself a meaningful existence.*

She straightened her back, took off her faded blue sweatband and tossed it on the love seat next to a Raggedy Ann doll and a textbook of typefaces. She marched into the bathroom, turned on the ancient shower, which rumbled dramatically but had a powerful, stinging spray, and began to strip off her perspiration-soaked clothing. Her body throbbed and her feet stung. She hoped she hadn't run so hard that she'd injured them. Running, she realized, could be an addiction, just like alcohol or drugs, and she never wanted to be the kind of person who became addicted to anything. That was unreasonably irrational, and above all else, Jana loathed the irrational—such as love, which was supremely irrational.

Already the steam from the shower was beginning to gently fog the edges of the full-length mirror on the back of the bathroom door. Jana judged herself critically in the dimming mirror, but what she saw was acceptable. A tanned little body, lithe, with a runner's muscle, breasts neither too large nor too small, hips and legs tightened with exercise. The face, too, was passable, clear skinned, honeyed with the sun, vibrant with health and not a trace of makeup. The only thing she found fault with was the hair, which was dark and too curly, falling to her shoulders now in a limp cascade from the perspiration of running four miles. And, of course, the eyes. The cloudy mirror gave those eyes back to her without distortion or pity—the startling blue eyes of her father, Kevin O'Dwyer, eyes the color of cursed jewels.

*No,* she thought, *eyes are eyes. Don't think of him. Don't think about anything.*

She stepped into the assault of the shower and let the pounding water wash her clean of memory.

When she emerged, tingling, she had only one regret—that she had been so rude to the man next door. For, after all, she had stupidly, her mind on other things, run into him. That he was rude himself was undeniable, but he had reason. She had maimed and probably killed his typewriter, and as a journalism person, part-time writer and full-time academic, she knew that a good typewriter could be the equivalent of a good horse to a cowboy.

But he was a disturbing man, and now, cleansed by the shower, Jana realized almost humorously what was disturbing about him. It was his maleness and the aura he gave of being so damned proud of that maleness. It was something her father had had, a sort of dubious magic that could dazzle the eyes and mind and heart of anyone subjected to it. She supposed some might call it sex appeal, and some might find it irresistible, but she knew it, instinctively, as a quality to be avoided.

Her own rudeness had made that a certainty. He was a hellishly attractive man, the sort to turn most women into warm gelatin. But Jana, by insulting him, had made certain he would never try to exercise his spurious charm on her.

She put on fresh clothes and went into the tiny kitchen to make herself a salad. She felt like herself again, Jana Fitzgerald, ordinary person, worthwhile individual, in control of a life some might say was so controlled it was boring. But, she thought, peppering her salad, a life that was predictable was not the same as a life that was boring. She had known an unpredictable life far better than she had ever wanted. And she had changed all that. Now she lived an orderly life. She would always live an orderly life, here in the pure, windy, open landscape of middle America, where life was meant to be as orderly and disciplined and pure as the clean sharp winds that swept it each long winter.

She was so convinced of the truth of this that she did not know why she awoke in the lightless hour of the morning, feeling lost as a child alone on a sea with no sign of life. It seemed a long time before she fell asleep again, and when she did, she dreamed she was in Egypt with Les. As they tried to cross a desert, the camel spat on him, and both of them were stalked by a panther, dark as an Egyptian midnight, with relentless golden eyes.

# CHAPTER TWO

THE NEW NEIGHBOR was not only disconcerting, Jana discovered ruefully, but he had a dog almost as irritating as he was. A large gray-and-brown beast that looked like some sort of mongrel police dog, it danced around on its chain like a thing possessed. Perhaps it—or the man—had some mistaken conception that the animal was a watchdog. If so, it was the most paranoid watchdog that Jana had ever seen, or rather heard.

The dog barked, woofed, yipped, bayed or howled at everything—the mailman, the garbage collectors, people walking by, cyclists, cats, squirrels, birds, and Jana noticed with amazed disgust that one time the thing sat down in the backyard and seemed to bark at the empty sky.

Several times she saw the man unchain the creature and romp roughly with it. The two wrestled, rolling on the ground, or played an elaborate game with a chewed-up Frisbee. Once the beast overshot its mark trying to catch the Frisbee and came crashing over Jana's hedge, landing smack in the middle of her herb garden. Crazed with the wonder of it all, the dog spun in violent circles, scratching and kicking up soil before it gathered itself and soared back over the hedge to slather its laughing owner with wild kisses.

Jana sighed. To complain at this point would probably be to declare an all-out war. She prayed fervently that someone else would complain about the dog, and had fantasies about a battalion of animal-control officers leading the man and his wretched dog to a paddy wagon.

The town was certainly lively enough to give the dog ample opportunity to bark. The streets swarmed with students, the lawns of the sorority and fraternity houses were filled with people spilling out from the parties inside. The streets were jammed with traffic, and radios and stereos seemed to blare from everywhere. All over campus a haze of blue seemed to have descended, as everyone sported Eastern's blue and white colors—in T-shirts, shorts, jackets, caps, overalls, even socks. Versions of Eastern's mascot, a strutting chesty blue-and-white panther, stared from store windows, and even the florist shops' display windows were banked with cascades of blue and white flowers.

For with the students' return, something electric charged the campus and the little city of Charleston. Excitement and gaiety seemed to crackle in the still-warm autumn air, and Jana loved this time of year most of all. Autumn, not spring, seemed the beginning of new growth as anticipation fairly pulsed in the atmosphere, bright as the foliage that was beginning to flame.

Jana steeled herself not to let anything dampen the festive mood she shared with the city, but she knew her determination was going to be sorely tested this year. First there was the new neighbor with that noise machine he called a dog. Then there was Zack Devlin to deal with for the whole semester, until Les returned from Egypt. Not that she planned to associate with the man any more than she had to. He was the kind of journalist she most despised, merely a high-class version of those who had hounded her family and created the carnival of pain and publicity that had hurt so many. And, she reminded herself, if Devlin hadn't been hired, she herself would be teaching the courses that were now his, and she had hungered for that experience.

Still, she had to be civil to Devlin. She was a professional, and she didn't take out personal grudges on her fellows. Besides that, fate, in one of its smaller dances of irony, had placed Jana at the head of the department's social committee. It was she who was in charge of planning the reception tonight for Devlin at the Arts Center.

Jana readied herself for the reception, trying to keep nasty thoughts from her mind. Nasty thoughts such as the one that if Devlin had been only an ordinary visiting professor, nobody would have bothered with a special reception; he would have had to take his chances at the annual newcomers' party like all the other new faculty members. But Devlin was famous and Jana knew, to her sorrow, that fame did funny things to people's heads. One might be the most odious person in the world, but if one were famous, people were in awe.

She heaped her dark curls on top of her head to give her added height, sighing as she did so. No matter how carefully she pinned the thick mass of shining hair into place, hoping to look dignified and possibly even severe, her locks had ideas of their own and soon would be escaping in tendrils that made her look like one of those winsome drawings of Gibson Girls.

She applied a gloss of rosiness to her lips, but no other makeup. Her dark brows and lashes needed no enhancement, and her clear tanned skin would only have been dimmed by foundation or powder.

She gave an involuntary shiver of pleasure as she donned her lacy underthings and the wisp of a slip.

Filmy lingerie was her one perfectly irrational weakness, and she took unaccountable pleasure from it. The dress she'd bought for the reception was not nearly as feminine and frivolous as the underthings it would hide. A shirtwaist of azure raw silk, it had an understated elegance that she enhanced by adding only a string of pearls and matching earrings. Blue high-heeled sandals matched the dress perfectly, and as she slipped them on her narrow feet, she welcomed the extra inches of height they gave her.

The only thing she hated about the heels was the anything-but-brisk way they forced her to walk. She smiled at the idea of striding up to the Arts Center in her running shoes, her precariously high-heeled shoes dangling from her hand. *Why not*, she thought. She had to look respectable at the reception, but in transit she might as well be comfortable. She removed the heels and laced up her tattered running shoes. She might look bizarre, but at least she could stride up to the campus at her normal pace.

She donned a shawl of antique lace she had indulged in on one of her antique-shopping sprees, picked up her small blue evening purse in one hand and took the sandals, dangling by their silky straps, in the other. Locking the door behind her, she took a deep breath of the misty autumn air and started out.

*Drat*, she thought. Her neighbour was in his side yard, playing with that monstrous excuse for a dog. She'd ignore him. But suddenly she wished she wasn't all dressed up and padding toward campus in ragged running shoes.

While she was successfully ignoring the tall man and the romping dog, they did not choose to ignore her. At least the great galumphing animal didn't. She heard the pounding of its feet behind her and a harsh cry of "Sasha! Sash! Stop, you blithering twit!"

Jana whirled around a took a step backward, alarmed. The big dog was bearing down on her, making a weird noise that Jana felt certain was a death snort at the very least. The thing leaped at her, a crazed look in its eyes—eyes as yellow as those of its master, who was now also bearing down on Jana.

The dog, Jana could almost have sworn, seemed to be smiling at her as it seized one of her shoes between its great jaws and began tugging, now making a sound that was undoubtedly the growl it made immediately before it tore its victim's throat.

The harder Jana struggled to pull the shoe away, the harder the dog pulled, crouching now, its big tail waving madly and its yellow eyes still gleaming with that insane smile.

"Sasha!" its master bellowed, grabbing the beast by its collar. "Let go of the shoes, lady! She thinks it's a game. Let go!"

"I will not!" Jana snapped, with more courage than she felt. "Those are my good shoes!"

"Let go, dammit," he said tugging on the dog's collar.

"Make *it* let go!" Jana returned. "Make it mind!"

The dog's rear end was describing a hysterical circle as it tried to decide whether to wag or sink its tail between its legs. Its pointed ears were flipped back, its eyes looked even wilder, but still it refused to release the shoe.

"Lady—" the dark-haired man warned, just as the dog gave one last mighty pull, jerking the shoe loose from Jana's grip, causing her to tumble backward, landing on her seat in the grass.

"Oh!" She had landed hard and her hair was spilling into her eyes. "Oh!" she repeated, too enraged to find any other word.

Now the dog was on its back, wiggling like one possessed, joyfully munching the shoe.

"Sash!" the man roared, and the dog rolled over, groveling in a parody of apology.

"Sash!" he thundered again. Mournfully the dog released the sandal, which now resembled something that had lost a battle with a chain saw.

"Here," the man said gruffly, extending her a hand and pulling her roughly to her feet. Jana stood, her face burning with indignation, and snatched her hand from his as if from an open flame.

With an angry movement he reached down and scooped the huge dog up by the scruff of its neck and shook it until its eyes rolled in terror and remorse. "You wigged-out wench!" he stormed, and the dog yelped its protest. "You vegetable brain!" The dog emitted a whoop of fear, and he set it down roughly, then bent and retrieved the shoe. He handed it to Jana, a look of disgust darkening his face.

She snatched the ruined shoe from him and considered flinging it back in his face. "Really!" she snapped furiously. "You...." But words to elucidate her outrage still escaped her, perhaps fortunately.

"I told you to let go," he said, crossing his arms over his chest and staring down at her. One eyebrow was cocked and the dark mustache seemed to twitch with disdain above the chiseled lips.

"If," Jana said icily, "you cannot make a dog behave, you should not own a dog."

"If," he said with equal precision and control, "you cannot react sensibly in a crisis, perhaps you should not be allowed to walk the streets without a keeper."

"My shoe is ruined," she said. She felt herself squaring her jaw and knew she was only one step from losing control completely. "I was on my way to an important engagement, and now, thanks to you and that—that—*thing*—I'm going to be late. Thanks ever so much."

To her dismay he threw back his head and laughed. The dog peeped up at him as if it, too, was bewildered.

"This is not funny!" Jana stamped her foot on the sidewalk, then immediately regretted the childish gesture.

"Hey, cheer up!" he said, laughing, the black eyebrow cocked even more rakishly. "Don't you see what this proves? There's justice in the world, my dear. You ruin my day and my typewriter, and Sash and I ruin your evening and your shoe. What could be fairer? Besides, you did look quite funny, you know, tussling in full evening dress, trying to keep your shoe and your dignity."

"I'm sure it was amusing for you but I can think of better evening activities than pulling my good sandal from a wild animal's jaw," she replied furiously.

"Sorry, but you did look funny. Poor Sasha has a bit of a shoe fetish. She thinks tug-of-war with a shoe is the world's greatest sport, and it puzzles her mightily that it's not an official Olympic event. She'll never let go. Never."

"You both ought to be locked up," Jana said, sick of the conversation. "The dog is as ill-mannered as you are. I see no humor in this, nor do I have patience with bad little boys and their dogs."

Seldom had she known such anger. Then, with a sickening lurch she realized how much she hated looking foolish in this man's eyes, though why she should care she couldn't imagine.

"You dwell in the land of illusion," he said, still smiling. "This is not a question of a boy and his dog. This is a matter of a man and his wolf. There's a great difference, you see."

"Wolf!" Jana's eyes widened. She looked down at Sasha, still lying, repentent, at the man's feet, ears pinned back, pale eyes watchful. "You have a *wolf* you allow to run loose and attack unsuspecting citizens? Of all the irresponsible—"

"Actually only half wolf," he said grinning so that the dimples on each side of his mustache deepened. "Her daddy was a German shepherd of an unassailably fine background. Her mother, however, is a Siberian timber wolf, the pet of a friend of mine. Sasha, you've probably noticed, has inherited her mother's eyes and her passionate Russian temperament. Emotional, these Russians. She'll brood for days about this, I assure you."

"If she comes near me again," Jana said, pointing her finger at him, "I'll make her into Russian salad dressing. You keep this...this werewolf...or whatever it is, away from me." She wrapped her shawl tightly around her shoulders, turned and stalked back toward her house.

"Hey!" he called after her. "Wear the running shoes to your soirée tonight. It's an enchanting ensemble—really! You look like Paris from the knees up and Dogpatch from the knees down. You might start a new look—designer gowns and combat boots, for instance."

She slammed the door, glad to cut off the sound of his insufferable voice. She stamped into her bedroom to take an inventory of the damages. They were extensive.

The shoes, of course, were completely ruined. A grass stain smirched the back of the blue silk dress, and unless the cleaners were in possession of either magic or true genius the dress, too, was ruined. Her hair was in disarray, and, in short, she looked like a woman who had just lost a struggle with a wolf.

A wolf! Really, the man was a menace. What sane person kept wolves? And what sort of man picked one up by the scruff of the neck and shook it until it lay at his feet like a lamb begging for forgiveness?

Jana thrust him and his wolf from her mind, and with almost military efficiency undressed, survey her frothy white underthings for damages sustained and found everything intact. She hung up the blue dress, took a clingy lavender gown that had a neckline lower than she liked from the closet and slipped into it. She didn't understand why she'd ever bought the dress, but now it was the only thing she owned dressy enough and had matching shoes—which she intended to wear, not carry, as she drove, not walked, to the Arts Center. She brushed her hair and pinned it up tightly again. Surveying herself in the mirror, she didn't like the high color in her cheeks or the fact that she was still breathing hard, which made her breasts rise and fall too noticeably against the low neckline. But she squared her shoulders and marched outside to her car, keeping a careful eye out for prowling wolves and her handsome, scornful neighbor. She just hoped he wasn't now out exercising his pet rhinoceros that just happened to charge anyone wearing lavender.

The Arts Center stood out from the other buildings on Eastern's campus. A graceful spacious structure of white brick, with clean dramatic lines, it was lower and more modern than the others. Inside it was airy and in possession of a simple elegance. Roger Boren and Nell Wickes, the two other members of the social committee, were already there, and Roger's wrinkled face looked pettish, while Nell fluttered about nervously.

"You're late," Roger grumbled. A bachelor in his sixties, Roger was usually irritated about something and had long ago given up any pretense of hiding his irritation, no matter how minor. "Nell's as fidgety as a filly in a stable fire, and I don't know what in hell to tell these Food Services people."

Roger scowled at the two men from Food Services who were setting out hors d'oeuvres on linen-covered serving tables. "I spent my youth learning the newspaper business," Roger said, his bushy brows drawn into a frown of impressive intensity. "How am I supposed to tell them anything about *canapés*? How am I supposed to tell them anything about the damned *punch bowl*? Where were you?"

For the hundredth time Jana wondered how Roger, the least sociable of men, had ended up on the social committee. "I had an accident," she said without apology. She was not about to explain to Roger that a wolf had eaten her shoe.

"I don't know if all this crap is right or not," Roger said, leveling a malevolent stare at the worker arranging tiny paper cocktail napkins. "It doesn't even look like food. It doesn't even *sound* like food."

The older worker, feeling on surer ground now that Jana had arrived, glowered back at Roger. "We happen to provide a very good catering service," he said, looking down his nose at the elderly professor. "We've had raves about our tongue cornucopias and our crabapple garnish. Our cocktail sausages rumaki are—"

"Horsefeathers!" Roger snorted. "Cocktail sausages, my foot. A weenie's a weenie. Devlin's a journalist, dammit, and one with hair on his chest. Who dreamed up this tea party? A bunch of elves with little wings? I'm surprised we're not drinking dew out of acorn cups or something. Zack Devlin'd be a lot happier bellied up to a bar, drinking beer and eating peanuts. I hate these froo-froo parties."

Jana gave the worker a conspiratorial smile that said not to mind Roger; he's eccentric but harmless. It was a smile she had used a lot in Roger's company.

"Now, Roger," she soothed. "Take him out afterward and you can belly up to the bar together. This caterer always does a beautiful job, and you know it. If things get too boring, you and I can go into the office and play gin rummy. You still owe me five bucks from the last reception, if I remember correctly."

Roger favored her with a wry smile. "You got lucky," he said. "One of these days I'm going to get you in a poker game and I'll win your whole year's salary."

"You're on," Jana said, giving him a crooked grin. "Now would you stop trying to give the caterers a stroke and see if somebody's around to turn on the sound system?"

"I can turn the music on myself," Roger said. "I don't need a custodian every time I want a light switched on. I don't know why you women are so in awe of anything mechanical."

He stalked off and Jana smiled at Nell. Nell replied only by rolling her eyes. Nell was a small woman with artificially blond hair and a nervous face. "That man," she finally said when Roger was out of earshot, "will drive me to my grave. Please, Jana, help me with these flowers. I'm all thumbs at this sort of thing."

Nell did indeed seem to be arranging the flowers to death. She stepped back from the two silver vases with relief, and let Jana try her hand at arranging.

"You look lovely, Nell," Jana said, admiring the older woman's gold linen suit that set off her carefully coiffed hair, a gray scarf at her throat picking up the gray of her large eyes.

"I'm not sure Roger isn't right," Nell said, her hands fluttering at the scarf around her throat. "Much as I hate to admit it, I just don't know why a man of Zack Devlin's stature is even here. I hope he isn't going to do some horrible exposé, making fun of us all or something. But why on earth is he spending the semester here? It can't be for the money. It's a mystery to me."

"Me, too," Jana replied, arranging the blue and white carnations and the fringes of fern.

"And I hope," Nell said, fiddling with her earrings now, "that he isn't one of those horrible macho types that Roger loves to think is the essence of *true* journalism. You know, the type who sits around all night telling you how, when he followed the combat troops into the jungle, he drank muddy water out of a helmet and ate nothing but raw lizards for three days. Or who thinks nothing's more entertaining than reciting how often and how badly he got drunk in Paris."

"Not to worry," Jana said, contemplating the flowers and cupping a spicy-scented carnation blossom in the palm of her hand. "He'll probably be civilized at least for the evening. And if he's not—"she gave Nell a mischievous look—"well, what could make Roger happier?"

"That man," Nell repeated, casting a furtive glance in the direction in which Roger had disappeared, "will put me in my grave."

"Nonsense," Jana laughed. "Everybody knows women are stronger than men." She often wondered if Nell, a widow of five years, didn't like Roger more than she pretended to.

The first strains of music came over the sound system and both women winced. "In my *grave!*" Nell said a third time, shaking her blond head.

Jana laughed. "Oh, Nell, go talk to him, please! Explain that Sousa marches aren't exactly the thing we had in mind for a semielegant evening. Get him to put on Vivaldi. Really, what a character!"

Nell skittered off, patting her sculptured hair with one hand, squeezing a handkerchief in the other.

Jana stepped back and surveyed the table. It looked quite presentable, she thought, the crystal punch bowl flanked with trays of appetizers, the silver coffee service gleaming, and the two vases of flowers at each end of the table. She was rather tired of blue and white carnations, but Roger, who was in charge of the social committee's purse strings, had a deal with the florist to get a discount on anything that was in oversupply.

"Looks fine," she said with a smile, hoping to cheer up the two workers from Food Services, who still hadn't quite recovered from Roger's criticisms.

The older one was mixing the champagne punch. "Who's coming that's got everybody so nervous?" he asked. "The President?"

"Hardly," Jana answered. "A writer. A journalist. Zack Devlin."

"Never heard of him," the worker said with a sniff, pouring the frothy champagne into the punch bowl.

Jana laughed and felt a perverse thrill of satisfaction. "Maybe you're lucky," she said, but immediately regretted it. After all, Devlin would be a colleague for this semester and therefore should be the automatic recipient of her courtesy, if not her respect.

She shrugged and for the first time looked at the rest of the Arts Center. Nell had apparently talked Roger into taking the blaring Sousa march tapes off the sound system. After a brief silence, the notes of violin music began to fill the air. Nervous, Jana wandered to the nearest wall to study the paintings on display. Vivaldi's music floated about her and she tried to force her mind to calm itself as she studied a large watercolor of a grove of birches in a gray-and-rose twilight. She couldn't overcome the familiar restlessness of a hostess who has everything poised and waiting, but whose first guest has not arrived.

Soon the center was filling with people, and Jana was too busy to think of anything except making sure all the guests were greeted and fueled with punch and hors d'oeuvres. First there was a buzz of conversation, then a low roar, as everyone caught up on the latest gossip and recounted autumn's favorite story—How I Spent My Summer Vacation.

Everyone wanted to know what she'd heard from Les in Egypt, but beneath all the bright and interested questioning, Jana somehow felt the pressure of unspoken questions. Face it, she thought. Everyone wanted to know what was *really* going on between them. Just how serious were she and Les? What did his going to Egypt mean? And when he got back, would he and Jana finally marry?

She answered the spoken questions, ignored the implied ones and sighed with relief when she saw Dr.

Caxton, the chairman of the Journalism Department, enter with his wife. The couple was alone. No guest of honor was with them.

"Jana!" Dr. Caxton said heartily when he found her. "Looks like a fine reception. Congratulations to the three of you, but you especially. I know you're the one who brings an aura of taste to these things."

"You also play the role of peacemaker, I don't doubt," said Mrs. Caxton, her dark eyes twinkling. "How hard was it to make Roger behave and Nell calm down?"

"Not hard," Jana replied, laughing. "Come and have some punch and what Roger calls weenies and elf food."

"Love to," said Dr. Caxton.

Dr. Caxton was a tall and stout hearty man with a ruddy face, a receding hairline, an impressive gray walrus mustache and a heart of purest marshmallow. His wife was almost as tall as he, with thick dark hair and lively black eyes that announced her Greek ancestry. "My great big gorgeous Aphrodite," Dr. Caxton fondly called her, so often that many people thought her name was Aphrodite, after the goddess of love, rather than Maude, as it actually was. They were a warm couple and devoted to each other, and sometimes Jana felt almost a pang when she saw how happy they were together. She wished her parents had been like that.

"So," Dr. Caxton said, filling his plate with the most fattening of the appetizers, "what have you heard from Les? How does he find Egypt?"

Before Jana could open her mouth to give her stock answer, Mrs. Caxton dug an elbow into her husband's tweedy side. "I'm sure Jana's sick unto death of answering that question," she said. "And that's not really what you want to know anyway. What you want to know is if Les and Jana are still a romantic item, if that's what they ever were, and that, my love, is none of your business. She'll tell you exactly what she feels you ought to know. And stop filling your plate with all those calories. You're on a diet, remember?''

"Oh, bother my diet, my love and my dove. And why can't I pry into Jana's love life? Whatever concerns my teachers concerns me," he bantered.

"A lady has a right to her privacy," countered Maude. "What I want to know is, where's the guest of honor? I know we're not early, so is he late? Oh, dear, I hope he isn't the rude type."

"I thought you might bring him," Jana said, glancing at her watch. "I believe he is a little late. Just enough to be fashionable." Inwardly she didn't doubt that Devlin probably was rude, so full of conceit he wouldn't bother with small points such as arriving on time for his own reception. Either that or just as bad, he was late in order to make a more dramatic entrance, a trick she'd seen done to death in Hollywood.

"Pooh," said Mrs. Caxton. "I don't believe in fashionably late. There are only two kinds of late—rude, and unfortunate but forgivable. I hope our arrival was in the latter category."

Dr. Caxton leaned over to Jana and spoke in a stage whisper. "We're late because my great big gorgeous Aphrodite here insisted on staying to the end of our son's little-league soccer game and the thing went into overtime. Hope we haven't inconvenienced you, Jana, being tardy."

"Pooh," Mrs. Caxton said again, giving Jana's arm a squeeze. "With all these people, who'd even miss us?"

*I would,* thought Jana, watching Mrs. Caxton's lively face. *I'd miss you a lot.*

"And Jana understands, I'm sure," Mrs. Caxton continued, "that kids take these games seriously. But I am sorry we're late, Jana. Everything looks lovely."

"I was a bit late myself," Jana said ruefully, wondering if she should tell them about her disaster with her perturbing neighbor and his shoe-eating wolf. She was sure they would laugh and convince her the incident had been humorous, but for some reason she didn't feel like talking about it.

She chatted a few moments with the Caxtons, then went off in search of one of the Food Services workers to see if they could supply any decaffeinated coffee for a faculty member who'd looked positively hurt by its absence from the table.

She located the worker, who was uncorking another bottle of champagne, cajoled him into promising to see to the coffee immediately, then turned to see Nell eyeing the gathering with a pleased but wary look. Her hands were clasped in front of her, her gray eyes shining shyly.

"Well, Jana, I think it's a success, don't you?"

Jana put her arm around Nell's slender shoulder. "Yes, thank heaven, I think so. I just wonder where the guest of honor is."

Nell shook her head as if profoundly puzzled. "Perhaps Roger caught him as he came in and they're in the cloakroom rolling dice or something. With Roger, you just never know. That man!"

She sighed, then turned to Jana. "I was so distraught over everything, I forgot to ask you about Les. Have your heard from him? How does he like Egypt?"

"He's fine," Jana said for what seemed the hundredth time that evening. "He says Egypt's very exotic and that the university's great and everyone has been wonderful to him."

"Well," Nell said patting the lapels of her gold suit, "he's a very nice young man. He seems so steady, if you know what I mean. Dependable. And so ambitious! My husband was like that, you know. He was almost made a dean. I really don't understand why he wasn't. Such a solid man. Some said dull, but it didn't bother me. He was stable. Not like some people I could name." She gave a brisk nod in Roger's direction. Roger's tie was already askew, and his white hair hung in his eyes. He was refilling his punch cup, and Jana wondered just how much he'd drunk already.

Just then Nell saw someone who'd accidentally emptied a plate of appetizers into a neighbour's lap and she sped off, clucking, to help. Jana decided she'd better start monitoring Roger's intake of champagne before he started looking for a lampshade to put on his head and began to recite "The Road to Mandalay."

She put her hand gently on the elbow of his rather worn sports jacket. "Watch it, Roger," she said. "Too much of that stuff and you won't be able to beat me at cards."

"This?" snorted Roger, raising the crystal cup with its pale contents. "Couldn't get a gnat drunk on this. I've tasted stronger lemonade. Hell, I've tasted stronger rainwater. Come over here with me. There's a painting I want you to explain to me. Nell says it's a work of genius, and I say it's a work of a chimpanzee having a fit. Don't know why they bother to build an art center, then fill it full of squiggles and smears and goobers of paint that don't look like anything on God's green earth except an explosion in a paint factory. There! Look at that slop!'' Roger gestured angrily toward a Picasso on loan from the Currier Museum.

Jana smiled at the painting, which showed a rather strangely shaped green woman covered with blue circles. "I think Nell's right officially," she said. "I agree, though, I've seen things I like better."

"Hmmph." Roger cast a look around. They were relatively distant from most of the crowd. "How's old what's-his-name, by the way—Lester? Did he arrive in Egypt safely, or is he still wandering around in New York trying to find the right plane? Not that I care."

Jana started the reply she'd learned by heart. "He's fine, He says Egypt is very exotic and that—"

"That cold fish? He wouldn't know exotic from a mouthful of mush. What do you see in him?"

Jana blinked, startled. She had to give Roger credit. He didn't hide his likes or dislikes, and he didn't pussyfoot around.

"He's a friend—" she began, but Roger cut her off.

"He's a friend," Roger mimicked, turning his piercing blue eyes on her. "Listen, Jana, one of these days I'm going to have to have a little talk with you. Advice, you know? As if I was your older, wiser uncle. I've been around, kid, and I can tell you that—"

But this time it was Roger who was interrupted. Jana heard Dr. Caxton's voice behind her.

"Mr. Devlin," he was saying, "I'd like you to meet two irreplaceable members of our department—our favorite gadfly and resident curmudgeon, Roger Boren, and our favorite professor of news editing and resident beauty, Jana Fitzgerald. Roger and Jana, Zack Devlin."

Roger leaned forward to shake hands, muttering crustily about enjoying Devlin's work. Jana had turned and now stared at the man beside Dr. Caxton, her mouth open.

He was a tall man of about thirty-five, with black hair, a dark mustache and hazel eyes that were almost golden. She felt a blush burning her face. Her neighbor. Her new neighbor.

He said something to Roger, then turned and extended his hand to Jana. He smiled at her crookedly, a deep dimple appearing in one lean cheek.

Jana tried to grip his hand in a firm efficient clasp, but instead Zack was carrying her hand to his lips, and she felt his mustache graze her knuckles.

"I believe I've seen you somewhere before, Miss Fitzgerald," he said, lowering her hand, but continuing to hold it. She tried to pull free, but he held her hand tightly, and she was not going to be able to snatch it back without seeming rude.

"How do you do," she said, feeling her heart hammering in her throat.

"Jana and Roger are two of the people who set up the reception," Dr. Caxton was saying. "Jana, why don't you introduce Mr. Devlin around. I'm sure he'd rather be in your always pleasant company than mine. Roger, what do you say you and I pay the punch bowl another visit?"

"I want to talk to you sometime, Devlin," Roger said, nodding curtly, "about that think piece you wrote on Cuba. Dead on, most of it, but you missed a few points."

Zack nodded back, smiling like a lamb, his hand still imprisoning Jana's as the other two men moved off.

"Ahh," he said. "Should we prattle of coincidence, about it being a small world? Or talk about something more interesting, such as Dr. Caxton's curious remark

about your always being—let's see, how did he put it?—
'pleasant company'?''

Jana stared up at him as if he were the incarnation of
the most humiliating nightmare she had ever had. From
somewhere deep inside her came the need and the
strength to fight the man's dominance.

"I think you're enjoying this all just a bit too much,
Mr. Devlin," she breathed. "Please give me back my
hand, and I'll find someone else to introduce you
around," she said icily. But despite the coolness of her
words, her knees were trembling, and her face still felt
scalded with embarrassment.

"I won't give you back your dainty little hand," he
purred, squeezing it so hard that she felt her knuckles
grind against one another, "lest you make it into a
dainty little fist and knock my block off." Then, staring with obvious interest at the cleavage the lavender
gown revealed, he said, "I like your dress. I'm rather
glad Sasha caused you to change your fashion plans for
the evening. You are now making revelations that are
delightful in the extreme—Ah, steady now, steady. I can
feel you trying to make a fist. Behave, my dear. We're
at a public gathering, you know. But you're right—I am
enjoying this too much. Promise me that bygones are
bygones, and I'll set you free. We don't have to be
friends, but we don't have to be enemies. We will be
working together, you know. Truce? Or do I have to
keep your little fingers entwined in mine all night?"

"Mr. Devlin," Jana said between clenched teeth, "I
would sooner cut my hand off. This is all very unfortunate, but please just let me go. I've already played
tug-of-war with your dog this evening, and I don't want
to repeat the experience with you. If you don't let me go
this minute, I will scream for help. I will say you're

making improper advances. I don't care what I have to say."

He threw his head back and laughed. "Improper advances? My dear Miss Fitzgerald, did you just escape from a Victorian melodrama? What if you did scream? What if you did say such a ridiculous thing? I would be admired for it, and you'd be considered a hysteric—the sort of sexually frustrated academic woman who looks under her bed every night, half hoping a man is there. No. I want a cease-fire, a truce, a mutual forgiveness of wrongs done. What about it? Or do we go hand in hand until this posh affair comes to its inevitable end?"

Jana's thoughts swirled, her lips trembled. "All right!" she said more sharply than she intended. "Truce. Whatever, just let me go."

"Promise?" he said, smiling down at her cynically.

"Promise!" she said angrily, trying to pull her hand away.

Still he did not release her. "Now, now." he said, raising his free hand in warning. "You mustn't jerk and struggle so. You fight things too hard. I don't want you to go pitching backward again and ruining a second dress. Certain things should be done slowly. Gently. With finesse."

She stopped struggling and stood perfectly still, staring up into his mocking face, and he did exactly as he promised. With an almost imperceptible lessening of pressure, he gradually released her hand.

"Now—" he smiled, cocking one dark eyebrow "—that wasn't so terrible, was it?"

She could think of no answer to give him. She could only stand, staring up into his inscrutable eyes, wishing she were thousands of miles away, a place halfway across the earth. Egypt, for instance. Suddenly Egypt seemed like the safest place in the world.

"I could," he said, smiling so that both dimples deepened in the leathery face, "teach you to do a number of enjoyable things, and do them slowly, gently, and with infinite finesse. It would do you good, I think, a great deal of good. I don't much like women who are always in a hurry the way you are. I'm not sure you much like being in a hurry yourself. What do you say to your taking me about to mingle, then we slip outside into the night and become better acquainted—slowly, gently, et cetera, of course."

The man, Jana thought, with a fresh rush of bewilderment, was really too much. After all his overbearing rudeness, was he now trying to flirt with her? She had no patience with flirts whatsoever, especially one so insolently sure of his charm, so unflappably certain of his magnetism. And because she found, in spite of his arrogance, in spite of his magnetism, that she was attracted to him, she found her defenses rallying, ready to fend off the thing that frightened her most.

"Mr. Devlin," she said sweetly, rubbing her hand, although he had not hurt it. "I'll be more than happy to help you mingle. But nothing else, thank you. I don't really think we have any more to say to each other."

"No?" He cocked his head and put his hand to his chin. "I think we do and that you'll be interested. Because you see, Jana Fitzgerald, I know who you really are. Don't open those morning-glory eyes in disbelief, my dear. I do. I know you, Jay-Jay O'Dwyer."

She felt as stunned as if he had struck her. Her spine straightened, the blood left her face. "I've never heard of Jay-Jay O'Dwyer," she said. She spun on her heel, went directly to Nell and told her that she suddenly had a horrible headache and had to leave. She was terribly, terribly sorry.

# CHAPTER THREE

"COME ON," Jana reasoned aloud to herself the next day. "So he knows who I am. It's not as if I'm Clark Kent and somebody found I'm Superman too. So what if people find out? I'm established here. They know me for myself. It's no big deal."

She was trying to revise the course outline for her freshman class, Introduction to Journalism, but she kept finding herself chewing on her pencil and staring into space. It *was* a big deal, and if people found out who her father had been, it *would* make a difference. She knew it.

A celebrity had once said that when you became famous or closely connected with someone famous, you didn't change as much as the way people's perceptions of you changed. Being the daughter of Kevin O'Dwyer, Jana knew, to a certain extent, that was true. People looked at you differently, talked to you differently, treated you differently. They didn't really see you, they saw the golden haze of fame about you. They viewed you as they might view a rare animal in a zoo. You lost the precious right to be an ordinary human being.

Worse than that were the questions inevitably asked once they thought they had penetrated your defenses—what was it like? What was your father like? What was Tish Farrell really like? Did you know her? Was she really that beautiful? How did you feel when your mother died? What famous people did you know? Was it true your father was drunk in his last six movies? How much money did he make? Tell me the inside story.

Jana stared, unseeing, at her course outline. What was Devlin up to anyway? She bit her pencil as she asked herself that question. How had he known? What did he want? Nobody knew why he had consented to come to Eastern in the first place, and ever since last night, she'd had a sinking sensation in the pit of her stomach. What if he'd come to find her? His business was digging up dirt, wasn't it? Could it be mere coincidence that he'd moved in next door to her? Maybe he was here to sniff out the true story of Whatever Happened to Jay-Jay O'Dwyer.

She threw down the pencil and decided to go for a run to clear her head. She must be getting paranoid. A person of Zack Devlin's stature wouldn't spend time down here just for her. She was a story, but not that big a story. She changed into her pink shorts with the matching T-shirt with blue forget-me-nots on the chest. She'd have to confront the man, that was all, and warn him to respect her privacy. She knew that celebrities like her father forfeited their right to privacy, but she wasn't a celebrity. If Devlin was up to something, she'd threaten him with a lawsuit.

She was lacing up her blue-striped shoes when the doorbell rang. Probably Nell, she thought, making sure she was all right after her dramatic exit last night.

But when she swung the door open, she saw not Nell, but Zack Devlin. He was wearing black slacks and a black shirt with the sleeves rolled up, and he was holding a cup. He gave her one of his wry smiles.

"You!" she said. "Well, for once I'm glad to see you. I want an explanation for that stunt you pulled last night."

Zack put his hand on the knob of the screen door. "May I come in?" he asked, already opening the door. "I come bearing explanations. I have so many explanations they drip from me. I'm a fountain of explanations."

He stepped inside, and suddenly it seemed to Jana that he filled up her little kitchen so much that he overwhelmed it.

"Besides, I've brought you something." He handed Jana a white coffee mug filled with something white.

She looked at it, puzzled.

"I'm lending you a cup of sugar." He crossed his arms and smiled with self-satisfaction.

"I don't need any sugar," Jana said, giving him a look she thought sufficiently ferocious to subdue him and put him in his place. "What's this supposed to do? Sweeten up my sour disposition? Look, Mr. Devlin, I'm tired of playing games."

"You're the most unappreciative woman I've ever met." He shrugged in mock disappointment. "I spent the morning wondering how to approach you. How does one make contact with a neighbor, I asked myself. I racked my brains. I pondered deeply. Then it occurred to me—I'd come over to borrow a cup of sugar. Isn't that how it's always done? But wait, I said to myself, that's just the problem. That's how it's always done. My neighbor is no ordinary woman. She'll not fall for ordinary ideas. So I decided that instead of borrowing a cup of sugar, I'd come over and lend you a cup of sugar. That's original, isn't it?"

Jana set the mug of sugar on her little wire-legged table. "I'm not interested in *original*, Mr. Devlin. I'm not interested in anything about you except why you made that ridiculous statement to me last night."

His face suddenly grew serious. The dark brows drew together. "All right. I admit. I'm trying to be cute. I guess I thought I could make up for last night. I'm sorry I miscalculated. I didn't think what I said would hit you so hard. You were just standing there, looking up at me and being so damned defiant. I just had the normal masculine impulse to take a little of the starch out of you. I didn't mean to hurt you."

She put her hands on her hips. Her heart was pounding so hard she was sure he could see it beneath the skimpy pink shirt. She wished her kitchen wasn't so tiny. She felt closed in with him the way she might feel with some dangerous animal.

He seemed to read her thoughts. "Look," he said. "Why don't you invite me into your living room? I feel like I'm in a closet in here."

"Come into the living room," Jana said. Her tone was curt. "Sit down for as long as it takes you to say whatever you have to say. And don't expect me to offer you coffee or tell you to feel right at home, because I won't."

"You are as forgiving as the average block of granite," he said.

He followed her into the living room, which also suddenly seemed too small. What was it that made this man so overpowering, she wondered, so much larger than life? She sat down on her red velvet love seat and pushed away an oversize rag doll that had been lankily lounging there.

Zack looked around, frowning again. "Well, you live in a doll-size house, with doll-size furniture, so I guess it's fitting you should fill it up with dolls. Where's a man to sit?"

"Dolls are movable, Mr. Devlin. Quite portable, really. Just pick one up and put it down somewhere else." She crossed her legs and arms as if in self-protection.

With ill-disguised distaste, he picked up Agatha, a doll in scarlet ruffles and lacy bloomers and set her on a rocking chair beside another doll. He lowered himself gingerly into a wine-colored wing chair like a man trying to ease himself into a piece of children's furniture.

"Do you only entertain midgets in this house, or what?" he asked.

Jana inspected the toe of her running shoe as if it were extremely interesting. "I'm not interested in hearing your analysis of the average height of my guests. Make whatever explanations you have to make, then leave."

"All right." He leaned his chin on his fist and studied her. "I know you're Jay-Jay O'Dwyer, no matter how hard you try to deny it."

She met his eyes and felt a strange sensation in the pit of her stomach. He knew. She could tell by the penetrating look in those strange hazel eyes, the set of his strong jaw.

"You are—or were—Jay-Jay O'Dwyer, and you think it's nobody's business but your own."

Jana didn't answer. She only watched him with great wariness.

"Don't worry," he said at last. "Your dark secret is safe with me—as the villain always says before he tries to seduce the maiden. I won't breathe a word of all this that you obviously find so threatening. And I'm sorry I brought it up last night with such abruptness. Especially after I'd just talked you into a truce."

His gaze held hers. She suddenly wished he wasn't dressed all in black. It made him look like a gun-slinger, a person of menace, although for once his eyes seemed kind.

"If you're wondering how I knew," he continued, "let's say that it's partly because my business is finding things out. I have lots of sources, and my sources have lots of information. Sometimes it's information I can't use. Something as simple as 'So you're going to Eastern. Do you know who's down there? Kevin O'Dwyer's daughter.' Things like that happen all the time."

"In short, the gossipmongers never stop," Jana said bitterly. "It doesn't matter that the horse is dead. They still keep flogging it."

"Look Jana, I wouldn't care if you were really the heir to the throne of Russia hiding out down here. I have better things to do than invade the privacy of young ladies who obviously value privacy highly enough to change their names. But there are two other reasons I confronted you with the past you find so distasteful. One is that it would have been less than honest if I hadn't. Through no fault of my own, I found out about you. If I didn't confront you with the truth, then I would have had to keep a secret, too—the secret of your...true identity—and I don't like secrets; they can be dangerous. Now we know the truth about each other."

He sounded sincere, he looked sincere, but Jana could not bring herself to trust him. Kevin O'Dwyer made his fortune by looking and acting sincere. Like

Zack, her father had been a handsome man of easy charm, and Jana had not been able to be near such men since.

"I said there were two other reasons. That was the first," Zack said, running his tanned fingers through his thick black hair. "The other you may find harder to take. And that is that I knew your father. I knew him rather well."

Jana felt as if someone had suddenly sheathed her heart in ice. "Thank you, Mr. Devlin. Thank you especially for your assurance that you're not going to hire a skywriter to fly over the state spelling out what you so flippantly call my dark secret. I'll trust you to honor that promise. In the meantime, I really have no time or inclination to sit around and chat with one of my father's old drinking companions. You may leave now. I think you'll be able to recall where the door is."

The kindness in Zack's eyes disappeared. His lip curled. "I wasn't one of Kevin's drinking buddies. I was one of the many people he helped. He wasn't Dracula, you know. He was a troubled man, but never a cruel one. He was generous to a fault—"

"Not to us." Jana bit off the words. "He was hardly generous to us. To my mother or brother or me. Oh, he gave us things, all right. He gave us pain and he gave us humiliation and he made his name into a nationwide joke and ours along with it. I don't want to talk about it."

Zack shifted in the fragile chair. He leaned forward, his hands gripping his thighs. He fixed her with a withering stare. "You're determined to remember only the bad, aren't you? That's not smart, Jana. He made mistakes, and he paid for them dearly. But believe me, the world's a better place because he was in it. I want to tell you that, because it's true."

"I remember only the bad," she shot back, "because there's only bad to remember. All the rest was false—lies. He cheated on my mother. And he did it so spectacularly that he might as well have put a gun to her head. My brother adored him—adored him! Am I supposed to forget what my father did to him? No thanks. I have no intention of looking down Mermory Lane with tears of nostalgia for dear old dad. Nor do I want to talk about him. If you'll excuse me, I was about to go for a run when you arrived, and I'd like to get on with my plans. So please go, Mr. Devlin. And take your cup of sugar with you. I never touch the stuff. It's not good for you. Nor is raking over the past. Leave now. Please."

She stood up, staring past him as if he were no longer there, but Zack was suddenly on his feet as quickly as a cat, his strong hands gripping her shoulders. She could feel the heat of his hands through the thin material of her shirt.

"Jay-Jay," he said intensely, "he talked about you all the time. You and your brother. He loved you deeply, you know, both of you."

"I'm not Jay-Jay any longer," she said. She stared up at him in defiance, but felt helpless and paralyzed in his grasp. "And he never loved anybody except that... that...*woman* he left us for. Leave me alone!"

"Oh, I'll leave you alone, all right," he said, bringing his face close to hers. "I'll be more than glad to leave you alone. Except, my bitter little neighbor, you who love to gather up your past hurts and gloat and glory in them, I have a promise to keep. Your father never got over the way you rejected him."

"*I* rejected *him*?" Jana tried to push him away from her, but he held her fast.

"It worked both ways, and you know it," Zack practically snarled at her. "You wouldn't see him, wouldn't speak to him, wouldn't admit he even existed. Oh, you were just as stubborn a little girl as you are now. You could have still had a father, Jana. He wanted you, wanted you near him as much as possible, but you'd have none of it. You could have had your father if only you'd seen that life isn't perfect and we don't get everything we want. Nobody does. But you wouldn't settle for that. Your father and mother were divorced—it's a thing that happens to thousands of kids. But they still manage to muddle through and keep on loving."

"Get out of here! Let go of me and get out of here!" She pushed against his chest and struck at his hand with her fist. "You don't know anything about it! Get out!"

His face was only inches from hers now. "He loved you, but he loved somebody as well. You couldn't take it, so you decided to hurt him back. And you did a helluva fine job of it, too. He used to tell me that if I ever ran across you, he wished I'd try to explain to you. He said, 'Promise me that, Zack, me boy. Promise you'll tell her I love her, and give her a kiss for me.' I've kept the first part of that promise, not that it's done any good. As for the second, darling Jay-Jay, I think this is going to hurt me a lot worse than it's going to hurt you."

He lowered his lips to hers with a hard fury, a relentlessness that ignored her struggles, until she felt so overwhelmed by his strength that she could fight no longer, resist no further. She felt as if his angry mouth were sucking the very soul from her body, as if a hot darkness were clouding her mind, drugging her into insensibility.

Then his mouth parted from hers and his hands released her. She felt as if her legs would not support her weight. She was breathing hard, and he was staring down at her with an expression she could not read. She felt a dim and irrefutable desire to slap him, but she could not even raise her hand. He stepped back from her.

"And now my promises are kept. Good day, Miss...Fitzgerald."

And then he was gone. She heard the kitchen door slam, and she put her fingertips on the top of her gate-leg table as if she needed to support herself to stand. Her chest heaved and so many emotions swirled through her numbed mind that she wondered if she was going to faint. No, no, of course not. She wasn't the kind of woman who fainted. She had never fainted in her life. Why hadn't she slapped him? Why hadn't she struggled harder against him? Why had she allowed him to say what he had said, to kiss her as if he was punishing her?

She didn't understand it, so she refused to think about it. She simply cut the thoughts off, neatly, cleanly, as with a knife. She had something important to do, she was sure of it—only, what was it? Of course, she remembered. She had to run. If she ran, she would leave everything behind. She would run and run and run.

WHEN SHE RETURNED HOME, hot, sweaty, exhausted, her mind felt clear again. Zack Devlin was arrogant, insensitive, a bully and a brute. She was not surprised that he and her father had been friends. Each thought only of himself, of getting his own way. She'd think of neither of them. If she passed Zack Devlin on the streets of Charleston or in the school halls, she would simply pretend he did not exist. She would will him not to exist with the same determination that had helped her survive so admirably up to now.

A magazine and two letters stuck out of her mailbox and she carried them inside, wiping the back of her hand across her sweaty brow. The first letter was thin, a request for funds from one of the religious organizations that Kevvie had belonged to several years ago. The second letter was fat, covered with colorful stamps from Egypt. Les, she smiled rather tightly to herself. Good, dependable Les. Perhaps she had treated him badly, never quite taking his proposals seriously. She tossed the letter onto the velvet love seat, promising herself to read it thoroughly and with full attention after she had taken an ice-cold shower.

Later, snug in her favorite pink robe, her hair bound turban-style in a blue towel, she curled up on the love seat and opened Les's letter.

The first part was filled with descriptions of Cairo, the university and his students. The second part began easing into more familiar territory:

By the time you get this, your semester will have started. The students will be starting to neglect all their other classes so they can grind out the best newspaper in university history, and Roger Boren will be terrorizing freshmen with his usual scare-the-hell-out-of-them approach. Roger is one colleague I most definitely do not miss, and on the day he retires, I'm going to dance a jig on top of Old Main.

And what will you be doing, Jana? Will you be thinking about what I said before I left? I meant it, you know. Some decisions have to be made, and you have to make them.

I think marriage would be good for us, not only on a personal basis but also on a career basis. I've been thinking about it for a long time, and I don't know if you've really taken to heart the significance of what I've said. If I could finish my book, it would be a great step forward in my career. I'm confident I'd be promoted to full professor. But to finish the book, I need time, and marriage could make this possible. I could take a year's leave of absence to polish the book while you worked. Later, you could take a year off, if you had the desire to work on some more of those little pieces of yours. Working together, we could advance ourselves.

Jana, I know this isn't exactly what you'd call a romantic letter, but you've made it clear often enough that you don't like that sort of thing much anyway, which is probably good. It's not my natural style, either. You know that I'm fond of you, that I respect you, that I find you desirable. I think you feel the same way about me.

We could make a good life together, and we both know it. We understand each other, and we're alike in many ways. I would like to be with you for the rest of my life. But I've waited a long time for your answer. I took this job in Cairo because it would help my career, but also because I hoped it would give you time to give the matter your most serious consideration.

If you don't want marriage, I can accept your decision. But I meant it when I said that I didn't think we should continue a dead-end relationship. I've reached the stage in life when I want a wife, I want a home, I want to think about the possibility of children. I want you very much to be a permanent part of my life. If you don't want to be, admit it to yourself and to me. You know how I feel and how long I've waited. I wish I could convey to you how often you're in my thoughts.

Love, Les

P.S. How's the celebrity Caxton somehow snagged to replace me doing? You could still knock me over with a feather about *that* appointment. Devlin has a dynamite reputation, though I don't know that it's really deserved. *Roses For Rama* was a fine book, but he's had two flops since then. Maybe he's through writing. I've heard he considers himself quite the ladies' man, but I'm not worried about you, pretty as you are. You've got too many brains to be impressed by that sort of thing.

Jana smiled to herself as she finished the letter. She refolded the pages and stuffed them back into the envelope.

Les was right—his letter was far from romantic. He wrote the way he looked—a little frosty. He was a handsome man, slim and dapper with hair so blond it looked silver, fair-Nordic skin and steel-rimmed glasses that made him look every inch the professor. People often said how dramatic she and Les looked together, both small and lean, he so blond, she so dark-haired.

But still, she could read between the lines. Les felt strongly about her. In fact, she knew one reason he kept pressing her to marry him was that he was tired of their rather chaste relationship. In fact, the depth of his desire had sometimes frightened her, but he'd grudgingly accepted the terms she'd set. She didn't feel attracted to Les in that way, but she supposed she could learn to. She would try to write him a long letter after she'd worked on her course outline.

She changed into a pair of blue slacks and a striped knit pullover, slipped into a pair of moccasins and sat down to revise the outline. She saw some important changes she should make, but in the back of her mind she was remembering the scene she'd had with Zack and the memory nagged her. She remembered how he'd kissed her, that cold, powerful, bruising kiss. She tried to thrust the image away, but it haunted her.

She was halfway through her revision when she heard a noise that was becoming irritatingly familiar—Sasha's mad barking.

A moment later, the front doorbell chimed, making Jana jump. If it was Zack again, she simply wouldn't let him in. But when she swung open the front door, Nell Wickes stood on her little front porch.

"Just dropped by to make sure you were all right, my dear," Nell said, smiling a little too brightly. "And I brought you a thermos of soup, just in case you still weren't well and didn't feel like cooking."

"Come in, Nell." Jana opened the door for her. "I'm fine. It was a sudden migraine, but it's gone now. Have a seat. Can I make you some tea?"

Nell settled comfortably into the same chair Zack Devlin had hulked in earlier that day. "Oh, no, no, no. I don't want to be any trouble. I tried to call you several times but there was no answer, so I thought I'd just stop and check. You know, to make sure you weren't in a coma or something. You can't be too careful.''

Jana smiled. Nell's world was a nervous one in which any disaster was possible. ''I was probably jogging or in the shower when you called. Anyway, I'll survive,'' she said. ''I'm just sorry I left everything for you to do.''

''Oh, I managed just fine. At least, I think I did.'' Nell nodded earnestly, as if to assure herself. ''Of course, Roger drank a bit too much and he talked the ear off that horrid Devlin man. They got along like two peas in a pod. Roger can be a trial sometimes, but he was really rather decent about helping me straighten up afterward. The man has a domestic streak he just refuses to admit, if you ask me. And frankly I think he's lonely. Though I don't know how any woman could ever stand to live with him.'' She rolled her eyes heavenward.

''You didn't like Zack Devlin?'' Jana asked carefully. ''Why not?''

''Don't tell me you didn't notice? Of course, you left so soon after he got there. The way he oogles women. I mean oogles and oogles them. Surely you noticed he was oogling you. In fact, I wasn't half sure he hadn't said something offensive to you. I mean, one minute you were talking to him and he had hold of your hand, and the next minute you were going home, with that sick look on your face. He didn't, did he? Say anything improper?''

So Nell had noticed, and if she had noticed, other people must have as well. ''Ogle,'' Jana said, playing for time.

''What?'' Nell looked puzzled.

"Ogle. Men don't 'oogle' women, they 'ogle' them."

"Well 'oogle' sounds nastier, and there's something nasty about that man. He looks at you as though he can see right through your underwear. But tell me, dear, did he say something to upset you? You really did look as if you'd seen a ghost."

Jana drew her legs up onto the love seat and hugged her knees. Nell knew something had happened, and Jana knew better than to deny it. "To tell the truth," Jana said, not adding that she was going to tell only a part of it, "Zack Devlin and I met before the reception. He's living next door in the Babcocks' house, and, well, we had a little clash before I even knew who he was."

"The Babcocks' house?" Nell's eyes widened. "You mean where that big dog is?"

"Yes, the dog was what we clashed over, partly. He doesn't control it very well."

"That thing barked at me as if it would like nothing better than to eat me up!" Nell exclaimed. "Expect a rude master to have a rude dog, I suppose."

"Rude?"

"Well, I found him rude, my dear." Nell patted her gold curls. "I mean he can be charming, there's no doubt about that. But when I asked him what brought him to Eastern, he shut up like a clam. And when I asked what project he was working on now, he practically told me it was none of my business! He said that he never talked about his work in progress."

Jana felt a familiar twist of fear in her stomach. Zack had said he had no intention of telling anyone who she was, but was he lying? Was he over there, in the Babcocks' house writing up notes about the scene between them earlier that afternoon? She could still remember the tickle of his mustache, and unconsciously she passed her fingers over her lips.

"And," Nell chattered on, "he didn't want to talk about his last two books, either. You know, the one about President Truman or the one about President Roosevelt. He looked positively *stormy* when I brought them up. Of course, I admire him for trying to write about such important subjects, but that's not his forte, in my opinion. What he's best at is contemporary subjects, digging deeply, exposing all the secrets, leaving no stone unturned, all that. Roger says he thinks Devlin's polishing a book that has something to do with the effect of fame on people's lives, but I'm not sure he really—Why, Jana, is something wrong?"

Jana had gasped involuntarily. Zack Devlin was writing a book on the effects of fame? Oh, no, she thought. He *is* down here to spy on me. He's probably going to hold both Kevvie and me up to the world to show just how much that whole circus of Kevin O'Dwyer and Tish Farrell had twisted their lives. She felt cold, almost sick.

"Jana, are you all right?" Nell asked.

"Yes," Jana managed. "Yes. Just my headache came back. I—I don't know what's wrong. Maybe I need glasses or something. I'll be all right."

"My dear, you're white as the proverbial sheet. You'd better take some aspirin and lie down. You must see a doctor if this keeps up. You can't be too careful, you know."

"I know, Nell, I know."

Nell left soon after and Jana tried to resume working, then tried to start a letter to Les. But her mind was wandering and she was unsuccessful at both. Next door Devlin's dog began to bark wildly, and Jana thought of a tall dark man who stood laughing down at her.

# CHAPTER FOUR

JANA AWOKE EARLY the next morning. Zack's dog was apparently trying to teach itself to yodel, and getting back to sleep was going to be an impossibility. Classes started in two days, and Jana wanted to be rested and well prepared. Devin, with expert help from Sasha, was knocking those plans into a cocked hat.

She rose and dressed in pale blue linen slacks, a white turtleneck and a blue linen waistcoat. She would go to her office where she could work undisturbed by the dog. She also intended to talk to Dr. Caxton and try to find out a few answers about Zack Devlin.

She left her house carrying her book bag. Sasha, chained in the side yard, saw her and began to strain at her chain, yelping happy greetings and wagging her tail madly. "Go chase yourself, you Siberian psycho," Jana muttered between her teeth.

The morning held the tang of the first September chill, but the sky was a dazzling blue. As Jana passed Old Main with its soaring towers, she heard the strains of rock music, and knew that the students were having their all-day rock fest in the quad before classes began. The air was filled with the festive restlessness of a new school year.

The tennis courts across from the journalism school resounded with the whacks of racquets against balls and the banter between the players. Buzzard Hall itself bustled with new life. All August long, when Jana had visited her office, she had felt as if she were visiting a tomb—dark, empty, echoing. Now the building was filled with the clatter of typewriters, the buzz of conversations coming from a dozen different places, professors wandering the halls looking for one another, students looking for professors, and custodians grumpily trying to change furniture and move filing cabinets about in the midst of everything else.

Jana got her mail from the box in the central office, then headed over to hers and unlocked the door. The journalism school's offices were notoriously tiny, but the janitors had managed to jam three bookcases into hers, as well as a pair of filing cabinets and typing table. Her framed degrees hung on the wall alongside a colorful poster of Old Main in winter, medieval-looking in the snow, its towers crowned with white.

Jana sat at her desk and flipped through her mail—the computer printouts list of students enrolled in her classes, a handwritten note from Dr. Caxton thanking her for organizing Zack Devlin's reception, as well as four separate mimeographed memos from Dr. Caxton, the usual opening-semester reminders. But one disturbed Jana.

It was the one that stated that all journalism students were required to attend a lecture the following Monday night in the library. The speaker was Zack Devlin. Teachers were encouraged to attend and to participate in the question-and-answer period following.

Jana supposed she'd have to go. She glanced at the other memos, then rose from her desk. She wanted to talk to Dr. Caxton as soon as possible, to find out exactly *why* Devlin had come to Eastern.

She moved down the hall and peeked in the door of Dr. Caxton's office. She raised her hand to knock on the doorjamb, but saw that Dr. Caxton was talking with a great deal of animation. Seated across from him were Zack Devlin, his long legs crossed, and a cool-looking blond woman with her hair pulled back smoothly in a sleek chignon.

Dr. Caxton caught sight of her and beckoned her to come in. "Jana! How are you? Recovered, I hope. Come in, come in. You've met Zack Devlin, of course. This is his agent, Christine Courteau. Miss Courteau, Jana Fitzgerald, one of our brightest young professors."

Jana had no choice but to step into the office. She offered her hand to Christine Courteau, and the woman took it in a surprisingly firm grasp, her eyes bemused, appraising. She scrutinized Jana so closely that Jana felt uncomfortable.

"Miss Courteau thinks we ought to tape and transcribe Zack's lecture next Monday night and the question-and-answer period too. She thinks it might sell."

"Not might, Dr. Caxton," Christine Courteau said, reaching into her handbag for a pack of cigarettes. "Will sell. It's my business to know what sells. I have three different magazines making bids."

"Just think, Jana, nationwide publicity for our students and our program. Won't that be something?" Dr. Caxton slapped his desk in enthusiasm.

"I'm for anything that helps the department," Jana said diplomatically.

Zack turned from Miss Courteau and looked at Jana for the first time, his eyes flickering up and down her body. Then she watched him turn to light the Courteau woman's cigarette and felt vaguely irritated. She supposed he could be polite, but the knowledge rankled.

"And I'm for anything," said Miss Courteau, "that makes Zack and me those pretty green dollars. Right, Zack darling?"

Zack resumed his stare at Jana. "I doubt Miss Fitzgerald concerns herself much with money or the other crasser aspects of reality, Christine, my love."

Again, the woman gave Jana an icy, penetrating look. "Pity" was all she said.

"I really didn't mean to interrupt your conversation," Jana said, anxious to beat a retreat. "Dr. Caxton—I would like to talk to you in private though, some time today. Pleased to meet you, Miss Courteau," Jana said, turning to go.

"Oh, don't run off," Zack said. He rose, and Jana felt as if he towered over her, his presence taking command of the office. "Christine and I were about to leave. And you do seem to always be running to or from something. It makes a man nervous."

Christine, too, got to her feet. She was a tall woman, dressed in an expensive suit of champagne-colored shantung. "Zack has promised me the royal tour of this quaint little hamlet," she said. "I'm a New Yorker, born and bred. I've never been anyplace quite like this. Do you know what I saw when Zack drove me from the airport? Pigs, live pigs! Fields and fields of them. Hoards of piggies. I must take pictures."

Dr. Caxton laughed. "Oh, Zack here's that folder you wanted—the tear sheets of Jana's work. I almost forgot."

Dr. Caxton handed the folder to Devlin, who tucked it under his arm, then put his hand on the back of

Christine's neck and guided her out of the office. "Much obliged" was all he said.

"Now, Jana, what can I do for you?" He clipped the end of a cigar and lit it.

"I never realized before that we live in a 'quaint little hamlet,'" she said, glancing over her shoulder to make sure Zack and Christine were out of earshot. "And what's this about my tear sheets? And do you mind if I close the door?"

Dr. Caxton looked surprised, but nodded. Jana pulled the door shut behind her and sat down in the seat Christine had vacated.

"Jana, is something troubling you?" Dr. Caxton gave her a concerned gaze. "You sound a little irritable. Are you all right? I was concerned when I heard you had to leave the reception..."

"I'm disturbed about several things. It's rather hard to talk about," Jana said. She took a deep breath. "Why did Mr. Devlin ask for my tear sheets? And why did you let him have them?"

"Jana!" Dr. Caxton laughed. "It's nothing to be concerned about. You know why we have the file—so the department has copies of every member's publications and so every faculty member has professional examples of journalism from his colleagues to show the students. You know the students are always a little more impressed by seeing the work of one of their teachers than of a writer they know by name only."

"I know, but—"

"Devlin's read everybody's work. In fact, yours is the last folder he asked for. He just wants to know the strengths of the other members of the department, that's all. If I'd known you'd felt so strongly, I wouldn't

have given it to him. But it's a little late for that now."
Dr. Caxton's voice sounded rueful.

Jana felt a little foolish, but she plunged on. "Dr.
Caxton, why is Zack Devlin here at Eastern? It's a
question I've been asked a lot, and I don't know what
the answer is. Why did you pick him to replace Les and
how did you get him to come?"

Dr. Caxton contemplated the blue cigar smoke that
rose from his ashtray. "People ask me that too," he
said, leaning back in his chair. "And I usually tell them
that I got him because I am all-knowing, all-powerful
and work in mysterious ways. But the truth of it is,
Jana, I didn't get him to come here, and I didn't ask
him to come. He asked us."

Jana blinked hard. "He what?"

"Somehow, I don't know how, Zack found out there
was going to be a temporary opening on our staff, and
he called me from New York and asked if we'd be interested in him. Of course I said yes. I was delighted.
And the hiring committee was eager to get him. Even if
he doesn't have a degree, he's got more than enough
experience and reputation to make up for it."

"But why?" Jana asked. "Why did he want to come
here?"

Dr. Caxton tapped his cigar ash into the crystal ashtray. "I don't, as the old saying goes, look a gift horse
in the mouth. I don't know why. I'm just glad he's here.
You, I take it, are not. Am I correct?"

"I'm neither happy nor unhappy," Jana said as
smoothly as she could. "I'm only curious."

"And a bit suspicious, right?" Dr. Caxton nodded.
"You're not the only one. The problem with running a
journalism department, my girl, is that you have to ride
herd on the most curious bunch of people on the entire

faculty—all these journalism hounds who sniff a story. What's he up to? I haven't the foggiest notion. Is he up to something? Probably. But he's not going to talk about it until he's good and ready, because he's a man who does things in his own way. Nell thinks he's going to write something terribly satirical about our beloved university and poke fun at us all. You don't think that, do you?"

Jana stared at her hands folded in her lap. "I don't know what to think."

THAT EVENING as she fixed herself supper, she could see through the kitchen window. Zack and Christine, both dressed in jeans and sweat shirts, throwing a Frisbee and playing with the dog. Sometimes the three of them rolled together in the grass in a mad scuffle. Sasha usually fled first, breaking free, running wildly in circles, then leaping upon them again for fresh assaults of play.

Jana was somewhat surprised. Christine had looked like far too cool a customer to enjoy rolling about with a smelly dog. Jana felt a twinge of something disturbingly close to jealousy. The trio on Zack's lawn seemed happy and complete, and she felt neither. With a sharp movement, she reached out and pulled the blind down, cutting off the scene. She wondered for a moment if Christine was staying in Zack's house but quickly decided that of course she was. What kind of an idiot would even ask such a question? Anyway, she wasn't going to peer out the window all night like some frustrated old maid just to see if Zack drove Christine off and deposited her at a motel, or if she stayed the night.

As it happened, Jana found out quite unintentionally that Christine did stay the night. Zack's dog woke her again with its barking and she stumbled out of bed, muttering all the swear words she knew. She put on the tea kettle, then jerked up the kitchen blind to let the morning sun pour in. She could not help seeing, across the hedge, Zack, barefoot and shirtless in worn, tight blue jeans, trying to quiet the dog, who was frenziedly baying at a squirrel angrily scolding from one of the Babcocks' oaks. Zack's shoulder muscles snaked under his tanned skin as he lifted the dog and gave it a shake. On the back porch stood Christine, in a champagne-colored nightgown and peignoir, holding a cup of coffee and laughing at him.

The two of them didn't show much concern for Midwestern morality, Jana thought, but in spite of herself she was struck by the power in Devlin's body. He had quieted Sasha, who now looked remorseful, and stood with his hands on his hips, gazing down at the dog. His broad shoulders gleamed in the early morning sunshine, and the golden skin of his chest was darkened by a mat of ebony hair that narrowed to a black line running down his stomach and disappearing beneath the waistband of his jeans, like a single black stripe on a tiger.

Furious with herself for admiring the man, she turned from the window and began making her tea. She put two strips of bacon in a copper-bottomed skillet, but her thoughts were elsewhere. She turned the heat up too high, and before she had finished squeezing the oranges for her morning joice, the smoke from the burning bacon began to cloud the kitchen. Once again, Jana voiced all the swear words she knew, snatched the skillet from the stove, stuck it on the wood counter and rushed to throw open the window and prop open the door to allow the greasy fumes to escape. Suddenly she was no longer hungry. She decided she would pretend to start the day over again. First—a shower to wash the scent of burned bacon out of her hair. As she stalked to the bathroom, she heard Zack's damned dog begin to bark again.

She kicked off her slippers, hung her robe on the pink clothes hook and slipped out of her shorty pajamas. She was ready to step into the shower, when above the hum of the water, she heard an enormous *thump* come from her kitchen, followed by a crash and a cry.

*What now*, she thought with irritation. She snatched a towel from the rack, wrapped it around herself like a sarong and ran into the kitchen. There, dancing on her hind legs, trying to reach the ruined bacon on the counter, was Devlin's wolf-dog, her tail thumping madly against the oven door, making a muted gong sound. The chair Jana had used to prop the door open was overturned beside the broken glass of orange juice the dog had knocked from the counter. With another crash, the skillet flew off the counter and the dog yipped as hot grease spattered her nose. A sooty puddle of bacon grease formed on the floor, and at that moment Zack came crashing through Jana's kitchen door.

"We've got to stop meeting like this," he said and made a leap for the dog. Sasha, ears laid back, gulped down the last of the bacon and simultaneously lunged past Jana and into the living room. Zack, barefoot, skidded on the hot bacon grease, roared his displeasure, and raced after the dog. Jana clutched her towel more tightly around herself and ran after them.

"Out! Out! Out of my house! Both of you!" Zack tried to tackle the fleeing Sasha, missed and landed full length on Jana's gray carpeting. "Out, out! Both of you! This instant!" she screamed, but Zack had picked himself up off the floor and was charging after Sasha into her bedroom.

She pursued them, and found Sash cornered—cowering on Jana's unmade bed, her back to the wall, her tail between her legs. Zack hurled himself onto the bed and seized the dog by her collar. "Ha!" he cried in a tone that made the dog roll her eyes and try to burrow under Jana's pillow.

"Get out of my bed! And get that dog out of my bed!" Jana shouted. "I'm going to have you arrested!"

"Ha!" Zack shouted again at Sasha, yanking her head from beneath the pillow. He gave the dog a resounding whap on the fanny that made her yip in protest. "Ha!" he said a third time, and swatted the beast again. Now Sasha crouched down on the bed imploringly, completely submissive.

"Out of my bed! Out of my house! Out of my life! Jana ordered. "Take that...that...wild thing and get out of here, both of you."

Zack, still holding the dog's collar, fell backward onto the bed, his head on Jana's pillow, his broad chest heaving.

"Much as I hate to admit this," he said, closing his eyes, "I'm afraid I'm going to have to ask for your help."

"If you don't get out of my bed, the only help you'll get is from an undertaker! And your dog from a taxidermist!"

"I am grievously wounded," Zack said, his eyes still pressed shut. "I am sorely hurt, my Lady Fair. In fact, I think I'm bleeding on your bedspread. I'm sure you're delighted that I'm bleeding, but not on your bedspread. Do you have some tweezers? I believe I may have sustained a mortal injury."

Horrified, Jana saw that his bare foot was indeed bleeding, drops of scarlet falling onto the pale blue sheet.

"You stepped on the broken glass," she said, feeling the queasiness she always did at the sight of blood.

"I also stepped in something damned hot, and I think I've French-fried the soles of my feet. Are you going to stand there or are you going to let me bleed to death? Wait a minute. Maybe I shouldn't give you a choice."

Jana hugged her towel tighter and dashed into the bathroom, gathering up tweezers, antiseptic, a roll of gauze, a box of bandages and a towel, which she soaked in cold water and swiftly wrung out. She hurried back to the bedroom, where Devlin was stretched out, Sasha licking his cheek in apology.

"Here," she said, thrusting the things at him. "You'll have to do it yourself. I'm not a nurse, and the sight of blood makes me sick." His dark lashes fluttered open and he sat up with a groan. "I think you'd better get a basin or something. This may get messy."

Hurriedly, Jana filled a clean dishpan with water and took it to Zack. "Here," he said. "You'll have to hold the dog. She may bolt again if I let go of her."

Jana wasn't sure she could hold her towel up and Sasha down at the same time, but she had little choice. She climbed into the bed beside Zack and grasped the dog's collar as hard as she could. Zack pulled up his bleeding foot and slid the basin under it. He picked up the tweezers and began drawing out shards of glass. Each time he withdrew one, a fresh trickle of blood stained the water in the pan a darker pink.

"I may faint," Jana said in protest.

"Why? It's my foot," he said. "Stop looking."

"I can't. That's the trouble. I can't stop looking."

"Then stop complaining. I'm not some Hindu yogi or something. I can't will myself to stop bleeding."

"If anybody ever deserved to run through broken glass, it's you," Jana countered. "I don't feel a bit sorry for you, you know."

"I'm only sorry I couldn't accommodate you by severing a major artery. I'm sure you would have found that a ton of laughs." Zack winced as he pulled another fragment of glass out. "Ouch," he said.

"It's what you get for bursting into people's houses like a madman." Sasha moved uneasily, and Jana gripped the collar until her fingers felt numb.

"It was a question of hot pursuit. All's fair in love, war and dogcatching."

"If you could make this...*thing* behave, you wouldn't have to pursue it hotly, through *my* entire house." Jana wasn't sure if it was the blood or Zack's closeness that was making her dizzy. If she stopped watching his foot, she found her eyes gazing at the ropey muscles of his back, as if she were hypnotized.

"If you hadn't burned your bacon, she wouldn't have come in," Zack countered. "Burned bacon is one of Sasha's passions. She sincerely believes that all the burned bacon in the world is rightly hers. Besides, your door was open."

He turned and gave Jana one of his yellow glances. She felt her head go funny and checked to see if her towel was secure. "My bacon was burned and my door was open," she said, as evenly as possible, "because I awoke in a foul mood to the sound of somebody's wretched dog barking."

"And I was taking her off her chain when she got away from me, because she wouldn't stop barking at the damned squirrels and I didn't want to disturb my neighbors. Next time I'll shoot the squirrels. Or the neighbors."

Zack wrapped his foot in the wet towel, but almost instantly the cloth began to redden in spots. Again Jana felt weak. "Maybe I should call a doctor," she said in a wispy, dreamy voice.

He turned his tiger's eyes on her again. "You're not going to faint on me, are you? You can't faint. The dog might get away again."

"You're losing an awful lot of blood," she said hazily, looking down first at his foot, then into his eyes.

"Oh, hell," Zack said, putting his bare arm around her. "Don't worry. I've got lots. Pints and pints of it. Look, are you all right? Put your head down or something."

Jana leaned back against the strength of his arm, closing her eyes. "I'll be all right. I'll be all right. I'm fine."

"Are you really? Because if you are, you should sit up straight. First, I can hardly pour mercurochrome into these gaping wounds with only one hand. Second, that towel you're so fetchingly draped in is about to come undone, and what I can already see is making my heart beat faster, and the faster my heart beats, the more plasma I'm going to pump out of my system."

Jana's eyes snapped open, she straightened her back, and her hand flew up to pull the towel higher over her partially exposed breasts. "I wish you'd stop bleeding and go home. Your girlfriend can play Nurse Nancy and hold your dog for you."

"I don't know," Zack said, his teeth gritting as he tightened the towel around his ankle. "I sort of like you doing it. Whoever thought that first day you ran into me like a teeny tiny freight train that we'd end up one blue September morn in bed together—with you naked."

"I'm not naked," Jana protested. "I'm wearing this towel!"

"But it slips and slides in the most fascinating fashion," he said, still holding his towel tightly around his ankle. "And me, with nothing on but these jeans and not a stitch under them, I assure you—"

"I couldn't care less about your underwear or lack of it. And stop talking like a randy tomcat. It's disgusting." It must have been extremely disgusting because Jana could feel herself blushing and breathing hard.

Zack studied his foot carefully. The red spots were no longer spreading. "I think you like it. I think you'd like me to whisper all sorts of suggestive things in your shell-pink ear. I think you'd like to feel my hot breath on the back of your neck. I think you'd like—"

"I'd like to see you in blazes! I'd like to pick you and your big bad wolf and fling you into the next state. I'd like to see you with your throat cut instead of your foot! And what I'd like most of all is never to have seen you at all. I wish you'd never, if you'll pardon the expression, set foot in Charleston. I wish you'd gone somewhere else to rake up your muck."

The lips beneath the black mustache curled in a mocking smile. "A muckraker, am I? Now that's hitting below the belt. What makes you think I'm here to rake muck, dig up dirt and go to the nastiest ends of yellow journalism?"

Jana's head spun. "Because that's what you do, isn't it? Dig up all the dirty facts?"

Zack's smile began to look a bit tigerish. "You obviously haven't read my last two books," he said evenly.

"Me or anyone else, from what I've heard," she snapped. "I haven't read any of your books and I don't want to. And if you're not here to write about something, what are you here for?"

The smile was gone and the eyes so close to her own went cold. "That's nobody's business but my own."

"Oh," Jana mocked. "Somehow you've managed to force your way into my house, into my very bedroom, tear up my entire home, but you can't even answer a civil question."

"It wasn't a civil question. And I don't have to answer it. I never talk about work in progress.

"And while we're on the subject of civil questions, let me ask you why the hell you are teaching journalism courses and why you have anything at all to do with a bunch of muckrakers?"

"Not all journalists are muckrakers, and I teach because I feel I have a responsibility. A responsibility to teach my students the difference between digging up dirt and good astute reporting—teach them to think before they write, think about whom they might hurt. Is that civil enough for you?"

"Yes, and pull up your towel. It's slipping again." Zack glanced significantly down at Jana's cleavage.

"You're an oaf," she said, hitching up the towel.

"And you're a prude," he said, unwrapping his foot.

"I am not a prude. You are a lecherous and suggestive man." She watched the muscles twisting like snakes in his back as he reached for the mercurochrome.

"You are a prude. You can't stand it when a man treats you like a woman."

"I am not a woman, I am a person," Jana said scornfully.

"You are a woman-person." He began pouring the red liquid into the cuts on his feet.

"Doesn't that hurt?" Jana asked, clutching her towel.

"It feels wonderful. Remind me to start every day this way. Of course it hurts. What kind of stupid question is that? And you're changing the subject, which obviously reflects your sexual frustration."

"And you're going to cure me? No thanks!" She regretted the words as soon as they were out of her mouth.

He set down the bottle and looked at her. "I wish you could see yourself. I'll bet you've never been in bed with a man before. You're blushing like a cute little octopus—octopi do blush, you know. Your cute little chest is rising and falling as if it were powered by pistons, and, in short, you're cowering there like a little bunny rabbit who's just been cornered by the King of Jackrabbits. You're practically paralyzed—half by fear and half by fascination. Your little heart is beating so hard it practically shakes the bed."

Jana inched backward, leaning against the headboard as hard as she could. "You conceited son-of-a—"

"Now, now! Don't use any words that would hurt Sasha's feelings. I'm not conceited. I fully believe you hate me with a thoroughness that is rather awe inspiring. But when I kissed you yesterday, I had the feeling it might have been the first time you had ever been properly kissed. And you could do with a great deal more of it. Not necessarily by me, although I think I could do a hell of a job of it. Why, at this very moment I can't decide if I should wrap up my foot or kiss you until you're insensible."

"If you touch me again," Jana said in a strangled voice, "I'll scream. I swear it. I'll have you put in jail for breaking and entering and attempted rape. I'll—"

"So I'll wrap my foot," he said, reaching for the gauze. "Your loss, I assure you. Oh, do calm down, Jana. I swear I really can feel your heart beating. You're making this mattress shake. With all that pent-up passion trapped in that small body, it's no wonder you run. You'd probably ignite like a firebug's wildest dream if you didn't burn off that energy somehow. What a waste. Pity."

"I hate you," Jana said, her throat tight. "I really do. I hate you. Hurry up and get out of here."

He knotted the gauze and tore it off, his arm muscles knotting as he did so. "My spectacular injuries are dressed and our revels in this sumptuous bed are ended. Of course you hate me, my dear. You hate me because I make you think. Think of things you don't want to think about. Your father. Your past. Your present. And of course desire. But I'll be off, my sweet, and you can go back to thinking whatever it is that you do allow yourself to think about. The weather, perhaps. How I'll explain this to Christine, I'll never know. When I left to shush my wolfish friend, she was reclining in her bubble bath, and I, her host, was a whole and healthy specimen with two good feet beneath him."

He eased himself to the end of the bed and stood up. "Aha. I think it will only hurt when I laugh. If you could possibly manueuver my dog in my direction, I'd appreciate it more than I can tell you. Be sure, of course, to keep your towel in place. Though I must say, from what I can see, you certainly have no reason to hide the remainder."

"I wish I'd let you bleed to death," Jana said, gripping the towel in her left hand and yanking at Sasha's collar with her right. Awkwardly she dragged the dog until it began to creep, its yellow eyes filled with shame, toward its master.

With an easy movement, Zack reached down and swooped the unhappy dog up under one muscular arm. Jana crawled to the edge of the bed and got off, standing up with as much dignity as she could muster under the circumstances.

"Please get out," she said.

"With the greatest of pleasure." He hobbled toward the door, but the bedroom was so small that he could not help but pass her more closely than she liked.

Suddenly he bent toward her, encircling her with his free arm. He kissed her swiftly on the mouth, then lowered his head and placed a short, burning kiss between her breasts. "Damned towel," he murmured against her flesh. Then, just as suddenly, he straightened and gave her a mock salute. "Somehow," he said, smiling at her furious blush and her two hands holding the towel tightly against her body, "I shall make all this up to you. Adieu. I enjoyed sharing your bed."

He turned his back, and the last thing she saw as he walked out her bedroom door were Sasha's yellow eyes staring at her in extreme puzzlement.

THAT AFTERNOON the local parcel service brought her a large box. Inside were a heap of richly wrapped gift packages. And inside the packages were a set of thick blue towels, a quilted bed comforter of pale blue satin edged with lace, and a set of blue satin sheets. The note read:

I said I'd make it all up to you. Am also sending a
man to clean my heart's blood off your carpet.

                    Love, Zack Devlin

P.S. Satin sheets are slippery. If you need another
party to keep you from sliding out of bed, I'm right
next door. The house with the dog.

Jana bundled them all back up and called the parcel
service to send them back to the store.

# CHAPTER FIVE

JANA WAS RELIEVED when classes finally started. The excitement and chaos of a new semester forced her mind onto matters other than Zack Devlin—at least for longer periods of time. The students had reluctantly stopped their parties and begun the academic year.

The campus became a sea of students; they could be seen everywhere, walking, jogging, running, biking. Upperclassmen sauntered with confidence and the freshmen, as usual, were easy to spot. Bewildered by the complex of buildings, the number of classrooms, they wandered, dazed, looking like people who had been dropped onto an alien planet. For the opening days, the most frequently asked questions on the Eastern campus were, Is this the right building? Is this the right room? Is this the right class?

Jana liked the look of her classes. She had a teacher's instinct that told her when a group of students would work well together, and work well with her. She was an organized and efficient teacher, and she would have been a happy one if thoughts of Zack Devlin didn't nibble at the corners of her mind, gnaw at her contentment. He disturbed her more than she cared to admit, and in more ways than she liked to acknowledge.

Since Devlin's lecture to the students was scheduled for Monday evening in the library, Jana had to call the social committee into action once again. Roger grumped and refused to meet them on campus. He was getting claustrophobia, he said. He had nearly been run over by bicycles twice, he said. He couldn't hear himself think in the student union for the damned rock and roll music. He couldn't have a moment's privacy in Buzzard Hall, because even if he was in the rest room, three freshmen would jump on him and ask, is this the right building, is this the right room, is this the right class? He wanted to go someplace where he wouldn't have to look at anybody under the age of twenty-one. All this youth was depressing him.

Nell wanted to have the meeting at her house and have tea, but Roger said no. Nell always nearly fussed him to death, he complained, and he hated tea and he hated little cookies. If they were going to have another blasted social-committee meeting, he wanted to go someplace and relax, and have a steak and a beer while he did it. Jana finally got everyone to agree on an early supper at the Lincoln Lodge Restaurant outside of town.

Jana herself wasn't happy about the meeting. She already had two sets of papers to grade, and she didn't like doing anything that required her to concentrate on the very subject she'd been trying to drive out of her mind—Zack Devlin.

She donned a flared skirt and matching sweater of heather tones, for the evenings already had a chill that breathed the first hint of winter. She backed her little blue compact out of the driveway, relieved that neither Devlin nor his devil-dog were outside, frolicking in the dusk. The traffic on Lincoln Highway, Charleston's central street, streamed with cars and swarmed with students on foot. Perhaps Roger was right. Exciting as the start of a new school year was, being out of it for a few hours might soothe the nerves.

The traffic disappeared almost magically at the city limits and Jana drove along the straight highway, enjoying the still-green fields of Illinois. Some people, like Zack Devlin, she imagined, looked on these plains with distaste, appalled by the countryside's emptiness, the flat land stretching like an endless sea to meet the immense horizon. But Jana loved the flat sweep, the tremendous sky, the feeling of freedom. During the warm months, the plains were a feast of color—the wide sky so blue it dazzled, the fields a crazy quilt of brilliant greens and golds. In winter, the same fields stretched dark and dead, sheeted with snow, but each spring the intense colors sprang back, and Jana was not sure that spring anywhere else was so miraculous.

The Lincoln Lodge Restaurant was a long, flat, log building, resembling a pioneer cabin with delusions of grandeur. Jana parked the compact and shivered as she locked it. Cold winds swept across the plains, and she hoped the brutal Illinois winter wasn't going to come screaming down on them early this year.

Nell, who always arrived everywhere early, was already seated at a table in the corner, inspecting the red tablecloth for pieces of lint. Behind her on the wall, a portrait of Abraham Lincoln stared solemnly down on the room. Jana seated herself, and Nell looked about the room with an air of worry.

"Where's Roger?" she asked. "You don't suppose he's going to be late, do you? I don't know why he insisted on meeting clear out here, anyway. It's such a long drive back in the dark, and the food is so expensive. This certainly seems an elaborate way to plan such a simple thing as making coffee for a lecture. I mean, we always do the same thing for these special programs. I plug in the coffee urn, and then Roger tells me I've done everything wrong and he unplugs it. Then, he fusses that I haven't put enough coffee in, that it won't be strong enough. I swear the man would be happy if we gave him a cup of tar to drink."

"Well," Jana said, "we have to have our ritual argument on the burning issue of whether we serve cookies. You know, the one in which you claim it would be barbaric not to have them. Roger claims nobody cares about the blasted cookies. I claim we always have this same argument and we always end up having cookies. Then you and I always end up making them."

"I would hate to taste a cookie Roger made," Nell sniffed. "It would probably be filled with bourbon. But really, we could have had this meeting in one of our offices."

"This does seem a waste of time," Jana agreed. "I have a ton of papers to correct. It seems lately we spend all our spare time planning parties for that...that man."

"My dear," Nell said, eyes wide. "Did you see that blonde he was squiring around? I'm sure that suit she was wearing was worth my month's salary. She looked like a movie star."

Jana tried not to wince at the word "movie-star" and was spared making comment by Roger's entrance.

Roger seated himself and glowered at the waitress who immediately appeared and tried to give him a menu. "I want a steak, rare," he said, waving her away. "And a beer, cold. And if a salad comes with it, keep it in the kitchen and save it for the Easter Rabbit."

Nell and Jana shook their heads and ordered the chicken divan.

"Really, Roger," Nell scolded when the waitress had scurried off, "there's no reason to be so rude. You and that Devlin man are two of a kind."

"I'm not rude," Roger grumped. "I say what I mean. And I mean what I say. And what's wrong with Devlin?"

"Well, he was in the hall today, limping as if he'd hurt himself quite badly, and I said, 'My goodness, what happened to you?' He turned around and leered at me, I swear, and he said, 'I was chasing a wolf across broken glass and landed in a lady's bed.' Then he laughed. I asked a simple question out of sincere concern and he had the nerve to give me an answer like that! Really!"

Jana's face burned and Nell's sharp eye registered the reaction. "Jana, are you all right? You're blushing like a rose. Are you sure you're quite well, my dear? All these headaches and such?"

Jana shook her head. "I'm fine, fine." Her voice sounded anything but fine. Roger shot her a glance that was half-amused, half-concerned. Surely Zack Devlin hadn't told him about that comedy of errors they'd played out in her house. But then, she would put nothing past the man.

"Let's change the subject," Roger said, still watching her face. "Whose turn is it to buy the coffee? Who's got custody of the cream and sugar? Have we got enough paper cups left from last semester? What's our plastic spoon supply like? Let's get all this ponderous business done so I can enjoy my steak."

Jana sat twisting her napkin in her lap. She decided she needed to wrest information from Roger if she could get it. "Roger," she said slowly, her face still tingling with embarrassment, "do you know why Zack Devlin's here? Do you have any idea?"

Roger's attention seemed riveted on the beer the waitress had just set before him. He raised it to his lips and took a sip. He shook his head. "I don't know. He's like a lot of writers. Closemouthed. You know. Don't want to jinx what they're working on by talking about it. He's obviously here for some reason, but it's none of *my* business."

Roger's remark, which hinted that Devlin's work was none of *her* business, either, was surprisingly gentle. Yet she still felt haunted by the sick fear that possibly, just possibly, Devlin had come to Eastern to dig out her story, drag out the whole tragic mess of her father's star-crossed romance with Tish Farrell again. But this time with a new angle—*see what it did to the kids*.

"Oh, come, Roger," Nell insisted. "You know more than you're telling. I know you and he go out for beers after classes. You don't fool me a bit."

"He wants advice on teaching," Roger said, giving them one of his rare smiles. "So who'd he come to for advice? Me, of course. The old master."

"You already told me you thought it was a book on famous people or something. So don't you dare clam up, or Jana and I will resign from the committee and leave you alone to plan this lecture Monday night, *and* the Christmas Party, *and* Les's Welcome Home Party, *and*—"

"Look! I don't know!" Roger took another sip of beer. "I get the impression that he's finishing some damn thing about kids in Hollywood, all right? That's just the impression I get. I also get the impression he doesn't like it much. It's just something to keep the pot boiling while he looks around for his next project."

The waitress set their plates before them, but Jana's appetite had vanished. Her temples throbbed, her hands trembled. "Some damn thing about kids in Hollywood." Her stomach wrenched. He *was* here to spy on her. To set her up, then tear her down. To open wounds that had taken so long to heal.

There she would be, in the pages of his book, her privacy for sale at all the bookstores. She wondered whose company she'd be in, what other children of broken marriages and Hollywood's bubbling pot of horrors, with too much money and too little morality, would Devlin expose, humiliate? Mentally she ticked them off—herself and Kevvie, of course; Margo Lansbury's daughter, dead of a drug overdose at seventeen—he'd probably like that one a lot; the Norris twins, one in prison for selling cocaine, the other a beach bum; Crystal Paige, whose father's box-office appeal hadn't been able to keep her from the expensive insane asylum. Oh, there were dozens of them out there—children whose only crime was that their parents were rich and famous and whose punishments were ruined lives.

The wave of sickness drained from her, replaced by a stronger wave, a surge of white-hot anger. The man was a vampire, a ghoul. His last two books had failed, so now he had a surefire vehicle, full of sensationalism and other people's pain. He'd tried to charm her. He'd tried to win her affection by claiming to have known her father—a lie, of course, she saw now. He'd even acted seductively toward her. What better way to get a woman to talk, to tell you all her little secrets than to get her into bed? He would stoop to anything, using his good looks and sexual power to get what he wanted.

Nell and Roger were looking at her again. With great effort, she took on an air of icy calm. She spread a piece of lettuce, wishing it were Zack Devlin's heart.

With elaborate coolness, she said, "It's Roger's turn to get the coffee, which really means it's mine, because Roger always buys something so cheap nobody can drink it. Nell's got custody of the cream and sugar. We probably have enough paper cups left over for the faculty, but with all the students coming, we'd better buy an extra hundred. Our supply of plastic spoons is currently nonexistent. Paper napkins we've got plenty of, although most of them are left over from last year's Christmas Party and say Season's Greetings. I'll take care of providing the decaffeinated coffee, but it's Roger's turn to scrub the coffee urn—before and after the party. It's Nell's turn to go to the bakery for cookies."

"No money for bakery cookies!" Roger said, hitting his fist on the table. "Why do we have to buy all these people cookies? Why should faculty funds go to buy the students cookies? They're like locusts. They'll eat us out of house and home. I'm in charge of collecting all this money, and people hate to see me coming to collect. We've got to be more economical."

"Don't expect Jana and me to bake them all again," Nell said firmly. "You always make us feel guilty so we end up baking these things ourselves, and I don't—"

"Who asked you to bake cookies?" Roger demanded.

Jana settled back in her chair. The ritual cookie war had begun. She could go through this conversation on automatic pilot, she'd heard it so many times. Her mind was busy elsewhere, planning to make this lecture of Zack's a very special occasion indeed.

FOR THE NIGHT OF THE LECTURE, Jana dressed in a slim black skirt, a matching jacket with cable trim, a high-necked white blouse, black hose and fashion boots. She couldn't decide if the outfit made her feel more like a gunslinger, a riverboat gambler or a preacher. She felt like a gunslinger, because tonight she was going after Zack Devlin with every intention of gunning him down—with words. She felt like a gambler because she was unsure how it was all going to come out. And she felt like a fire-and-brimstone preacher because she was filled with a moral rage against what the man planned to do to her and to the children of other celebrities.

The students were filling up the library lecture room, and when Jana saw Dr. Caxton ushering Zack in, she took her seat. Zack wore a closely fitting gray suit that emphasized his broad shoulders and narrow waist and hips. The girls in the audience stirred, purring their approval, appreciating his rugged masculine presence, the aura of almost pure sexuality that emanated from him.

Jana crossed her legs and prepared to take notes on the lecture. If he said anything she could use against him, she would not hesitate to do so. And she had done her homework well after the evening with Roger and Nell. She had checked all three of Devlin's books out of the library, had read them with her sharpest critical instincts honed. Zack Devlin had caught her off guard too many times. Tonight she planned to turn the tables.

Dr. Caxton introduced Zack, who gave the audience a wry smile, joked about having done his social duty by wearing a tie, then took it off and unbuttoned the collar of his shirt, revealing the springy black hairs at the base of his tanned throat. He talked casually about journalism, about his early experience as a stringer for a dozen California papers and about being driven to persist in a highly competitive field. His remarks were hardly what Jana would think of as a formal lecture, but, she noted grudgingly, the students seemed to enjoy it.

When he asked if there were any questions, some of the bolder students shot up their hands. Zack answered them, often with dry humor that made the audience warm to him even more. The man was no fool, Jana thought. He knew how to charm, how to manipulate.

At last the students seemed to run out of fuel, or more likely, Jana imagined, most of them were too shy to ask the Great Man their humble questions.

"No more probing, relentless reporters' inquiries?" Zack asked from the podium. Jana's arm shot into the air. "I have a few questions, Mr. Devlin. If you have the time and inclination to answer them."

Several students turned to stare at her. Zack quirked an eyebrow. "I don't know, Miss Fitzgerald. From the tone of your voice, I'd say you sound armed and dangerous." A few students laughed nervously, but Jana ignored them. She could not let anything rattle her. She needed to be cool and professional.

She took a deep breath. "You've written three books, the last two of which have been critical and popular failures. Why haven't you been able to repeat the success of *Roses for Rama*?"

Jana heard someone near her gasp. From the podium, Zack's eyes met hers. The lips beneath the black mustache curled in a sardonic smile. "Nobody bats a thousand, Miss Fitzgerald. We all strike out from time to time." His eyes flicked over her with an insolence Jana found intolerable. "We all attempt from time to time to bring some desirable thing to a pleasant climax.

In certain instances I've failed, which doesn't mean I won't try again.''

Jana set her jaw as she usually did when angered to her flash point. ''*Roses for Rama* was the exposé of the scandals and abuses connected with a religious cult. The other two books were about American presidents. My question is: do you feel your last two books, on serious subjects, ran counter to your journalistic gifts? That your strength as a writer is in exposé, rather than in serious analysis?''

Zack's pale eyes glinted with amusement. Again he smiled. ''Are you saying that I can deal with the sensational, but not the serious? That as a glorified muckraker I've made my mark, but I fall on my face when I go after bigger game?''

His refusal to take her seriously infuriated her. ''The words are yours, Mr. Devlin, not mine. But since you put it that way—''

''I'm only trying to help you out,'' he mocked. ''You seem to have trouble getting to the point.''

''The point's been made,'' Jana flared. ''You seem to make money digging up scandal, but your last two books—''

Zack cut her off, holding up his hands as if pleading for mercy. ''My last two books,'' he said, smiling wryly, ''didn't make much of an impression on the book-buying public. I regret that. But if I were doing it all over, I'd write the books again. It was something I needed to do at the time, as a writer.''

''The critics didn't seem to think you needed to do them at all,'' Jana shot back. She held a sheaf of notes in front of her, her hand trembling in spite of herself. ''Would you like me to read you some of your reviews?''

"Not particularly," Zack said, quirking an eyebrow. "I've already read them. Once was enough."

A few students laughed nervously, and Jana felt the situation was slipping out of control.

"Besides," he continued easily, rubbing a finger across the black mustache, "even if the books failed, I'd rather fail at something ambitious than succeed at something easy."

Jana straightened her back and tossed her hair. "Such as what, Mr. Devlin? What is your next project? It's been two years since you've published anything. Will you go back to what you do best?"

Zack's smile disappeared. His eyes grew stony. "I never talk about work in progress," he said.

"Why not?" Jana demanded. "Surely it couldn't be that your work is something you're ashamed to talk about, is it?"

His long fingers were clamped around the edge of the podium. The eyes that met her own were hard. "I never talk about work in progress," he repeated.

"Are you returning to your old style, your previous approach?" Jana challenged.

"I didn't know I had an 'old style' or a 'previous approach.' I just write," Devlin returned. In his eyes she sensed a burning warning.

Jana plunged on. "By your old style, I mean your successful style, as in *Roses for Rama*, in which you held up the sad follies of Rama and his followers to public scorn. In which you made a mockery of a number of people who were unfortunate but sincere, who—"

"Hold it!" Zack thundered, leaning forward. "I don't think you want to challenge my integrity any further, Miss Fitzgerald."

Jana felt desperate, like a person who is speeding toward the edge of a cliff and can't stop. The other people in the room seemed to disappear, leaving only herself, Zack, and a crowd of agonized ghosts—her mother, her father, Kevvie and the other children she had known in Hollywood whose lives had been destroyed by men like Zack Devlin. "Integrity is not a word I would use in connection with you, Mr. Devlin." Her voice sounded sharp as a slap, and as soon as the words were out of her mouth, she knew they were the wrong words, but she couldn't stop herself. "Your strongest suit seems to be mongering other people's pain, selling other people's misery—"

"Hold it!" Zack repeated, his eyes burning into hers. "I didn't tell anyone's story who didn't want his story told. I had releases from everybody except Rama, and he was in prison. What he'd done was a matter of public record. A lot of people Rama duped hoped that having their stories told would keep others from making the same mistakes. Rama's was only one of a number of dangerous cults that—"

"You make it sound noble—or nearly. But you're evading the issue. The issue is just who have you picked as the target of your next hatchet job, Mr. Devlin?" Jana's eyes blazed as hotly as his. Again everything in the room seemed foggy, unreal, except for Devlin and her own sad ghosts. "Are you incapable of doing anything except cheap hatchet jobs on innocent people?"

Their eyes locked, and Jana felt the charge of intense energy that reverberated between them. "Miss Fitzgerald," he drawled at last, still gripping the podium so hard that his knuckles whitened beneath the tanned skin, "your academic idealism is touching, but hardly realistic. I'm sorry you don't consider me worthy to speak before your students. Perhaps the students have found otherwise. I sincerely hope so. But I think I've taken a big enough chunk out of everybody's evening. And I'm sure I've been dry enough to make everybody thirsty. Let's call it a night and have some coffee. Thank you very much for your attention."

He nodded at the audience, raised his hand in mock farewell, then strode from the speaker's podium. The room suddenly hissed with whispers, and Jana felt eyes furtively appraising her, but she held her head up, chin tilted. She had wanted to give Zack Devlin a dose of his own medicine, the bitter medicine of public scorn. Yet the exchange had gone so swiftly she felt dizzy, unsure of what she'd said or of anything at all—except that burning line of intensity that had sizzled between her and the man who was stalking her privacy.

He stood at the coffee urn, casually filling a cup with the strong black brew, saying something to Roger. Jana stood up. She wasn't through with him yet. She still had a few things to say to Mr. Zack Devlin.

But Nell was by her side, her hands fluttering nervously. "Oh, Jana," she protested. "Do you really think you should have done that? I mean, you certainly gave him a piece of your mind, but do you really think you were quite fair? My dear, I mean..."

Jana caught one of Nell's jittering hands between her own and gave it a squeeze. "Nell, I did what I had to do. Believe me." But her head still swam, as if she had just run too hard, too fast, too long.

She saw Dr. Caxton hurrying toward her, his face pink with embarrassment—or anger. Nell scampered away to oversee the dispensing of coffee. Dr. Caxton took Jana's arm, shaking his head. "Jana, Jana, I don't know what to think," he muttered. "You know you're one of my favorite people in the department, but what on earth was *that* about? You have every right to your opinions, but I'm not sure you considered those opinions carefully. Zack Devlin's won some prestigious awards. You may not like his work, but I'm not sure you can justify attacking him the way you did. Jana, you're in journalism yourself—you know it's our job to be fair, objective, rational. And as much as I like you, I'm not sure you were any of those things tonight.''

Jana bit her lip. Dr. Caxton looked betrayed, wounded. She had set out to gun down Devlin, but the weapon had exploded in her own hand, hurting her and those around her. She felt suddenly sick at her stomach.

"It's also our job to search for truth, to set the facts before the public,'' she began, with a sinking feeling that she'd failed miserably.

But then Zack was at Dr. Caxton's side, his arm around the burly older man's back. With a panther's grace, he put his other arm around Jana, but the smile he gave her had a glitter of menace.

"She did a great job, didn't she?'' Zack said, smiling down at Jana—but the smile held more warning than warmth. "What do you think, Dr. Caxton? Was she convincing? We'll see just how good these journalism students are, eh?''

Dr. Caxton looked up at Devlin in puzzlement, his walrus mustache twitching as he searched for words. "I don't understand,'' he finally said, looking at Jana and back at Zack.

Zack gave Dr. Caxton's shoulder a friendly smack, then put his hand on Jana's upper arm. His other arm was around her like a band of iron.

"Jana and I came up with a little scheme to test the students' powers of observation—a more realistic variation, we hoped, of the old saw of having somebody rush into the classroom and stab the teacher. The students gasp, the attacker rushes out, the teacher explains it's all been a test and the students have to describe what they saw. Ninety percent will have been too caught up in what had been happening to describe anything accurately—including the fact that the 'attacker' never had a knife at all. He usually has something no more lethal than a banana.''

Dr. Caxton gave a snort of laughter. ''I don't believe it,'' he said, but he was shaking his head in relief.

''That device has been used so often,'' Devlin said smoothly, giving Jana another warning look, ''that we thought we would cook up something a little more realistic. How'd we do?''

''Too well,'' Dr. Caxton chuckled. ''I was just about to read Jana the riot act. I'm flabbergasted.''

''The students come in expecting to drowse through a lecture,'' Devlin continued, his grip on Jana's arm tightening perceptibly, ''and I gave them that. But we also gave them an incident, and when we ask them to write about it tomorrow, we'll see just how accurately they saw what they saw, what kind of reporters they are.''

''Unorthodox, but effective, I suppose. Do you mind if I tell the other faculty members? I was afraid Nell was going to have a nervous breakdown before you two got through slugging it out. And Professor Forstetter looked as if he was either going to creep under his chair or stand up and call for Jana's immediate resignation.''

Jana's knees trembled beneath her, and she was almost grateful for Devlin's cruelly strong arm around her.

"If you wouldn't mind telling them in private," Devlin said. "We don't want the students to catch on. In fact, I feel their bright little eyes boring into us this minute, so Jana and I are going to go outside to give the impression we are resolving our differences. In private. We'll be back shortly. Sorry if we gave you a turn, Dr. Caxton."

The older man smiled ruefully. "Jana's my most creative teacher," he said. "But this time she's outdone herself. My dear, if you ever give up journalism, you can go on the stage."

Jana flinched at the reference to her father's profession, and Zack's hand gripped her arm more tightly. She felt faint, bewildered. Why was he springing to her rescue? If it was another of his tricks, she wasn't sorry this time.

"And—" Dr. Caxton sounded hesitant "—since all this was an experiment, so to speak, it won't be included in the text when your agent sells the lecture, will it? I mean, since it was all set up as a classroom exercise, I don't see why...people might misunderstand...it might reflect poorly on the department..."

Devlin gave a good-natured shrug. "Christine said she could sell a lecture and a question-and-answer period. But even Christine isn't good enough to sell a goofy little play we cooked up over coffee one afternoon. All those remarks will be deleted. Don't worry about it."

Dr. Caxton shook his head again. "Marvelous," he said.

"Now Jana and I make our dramatic exit into the night," Devlin said. "Come along, Jana, and try to look like you're still mad."

As he began to steer her across the room, Jana's senses seemed to desert her, or rather fled to those parts of her body where Devlin touched her. She felt as if she had a live power line coiled around her shoulders that was jolting some foreign voltage through her.

"You little fool," he whispered fiercely in her ear. The flesh along her throat burned with his hot breath. "What were you trying to do? I hope you're satisfied. Next time you want to commit suicide, why don't you walk in front of a truck?"

"What on earth are you trying to do?" Jana breathed, wishing she could wrench out of his overpowering grasp.

"I'm trying to save your pretty little neck, my kamikaze darling. And I want the answers to a few questions. I don't know if you've finally jogged your brains completely out of your head, or if you've lived in your gingerbread house with your dollies so long that you've reverted to being eight years old. If tonight is an example of what you were like as a child, no wonder your father could never get through to you. I never saw such a—"

"Leave my father out of this!" she demanded. They were outside the library now, but Zack kept walking, half dragging her, half forcing her toward the deserted darkened quad.

"I'd love to leave your father out of it," he growled, stopping to glare down at her. Her heart leaped, fluttering in her throat. "But it doesn't seem we can, can we?"

# CHAPTER SIX

THE NIGHT WAS BLUE and strange, with the cold plains'
wind scudding twists of cloud across the moon's pale
face. Jana shivered, wishing Zack would release his hold
on her. His nearness sent a confused message rushing
through her body that tingled more than the kiss of the
night wind. Beside them, in the flower beds of the quad,
dead flowers rattled dryly, chattering brokenly about
the autumn chill.

The uneasy moonlight played across Zack's craggy
features as he bent above her, the shadowed lines of his
face harsh. "You really were a little fool in there," he
growled, shaking her arm. Jana refused to meet his
eyes. He was trying to overpower her, hypnotize her,
suck her soul from her body. She stared away from him,
up at the turrets of Old Main, spectral in the shifting
light. She thought absurdly of the princess she had always imagined prisoned in its highest turret.

Devlin shook her again, more roughly this time.
"What were you trying to do in there? Not to me—to
yourself? Don't you realize how you sounded?" He
took her chin between his thumb and forefinger and
forced her face to raise to his.

"Let go of me," she said, pushing against his hard-
muscled chest, but his strength made a mockery of her
struggles.

"Don't you know how you sounded?" he snapped, bringing his face closer to hers. "Don't you realize?"

"I don't care!" she hurled back. "I don't care what I sounded like! I wanted to stop you and I wanted you to have a taste of your own medicine! Let go of me!" She thrust her arms impotently against the wall of his chest again.

"Stop struggling, Jana," he ordered, pulling her closer with one relentless arm, while his other hand flew to her wrists, imprisoning them. "At best, someone will think we're having a lovers' quarrel, and at worst that I'm trying to rape you. Right now we're simply two people who've had a nasty run-in in a lecture room— let's not end up on the police blotter as well."

"Take your hands off me!" she breathed, but her body went still against his. "Who do you think you are?"

"Ah, better," he said, his breath warm on her chilled face, his grip still tight. "The question is not who *I* am, you little hellcat, it's who do you think *you* are, pulling a stunt like that? What do you mean, you want to stop me, give me a taste of my own medicine? What were you trying to do in there?"

Jana felt the icy surge of her old anger flow through her veins, giving her strength. The entire night seemed to be turning to ice around her, except for Devlin's hot hand like a band of flame around her wrists. "Don't pretend you don't know! You're hardly the type to play innocent! What I mean is that I won't let you do it. I know something about the law. You're not going to dig up the old scandals again. Enough people have been hurt. You're not going to hurt them again—not me or Kevvie or anyone else. Don't think I can't fight back. If you try to publish your seamy little exposé, I'll block you. I'll fight you in court until you quit or until hell freezes over, whichever comes first! Writing about Rama was one thing, but dredging up the old pain of wounded children is another. And you'll only do it over my dead body."

His tall form went still as stone. He straightened up, staring down at her. His face was hidden by shadows. She stood, quivering, her chin raised in defiance.

"Oh, Jana," he said, his voice edged with hardness. "You're a greater fool than I thought." He shook his head and laughed, a dry, humorless laugh. "I see now. You think I'm here at Eastern to write about you?" His voice taunted her.

"I know you are," she said between her teeth, but something in him frightened her.

"So that's the bee in your bonnet and the bat in your belfry," he scoffed. "Don't you think that's just a bit conceited of you? Your ego may rival your father's, my dear."

"Don't deny it!" Jana retorted, stiffening, wishing he wasn't so disturbingly close to her, confusing her senses.

"I deny it, I refute it and I reject it," Zack said, disgust in his voice. "You really think I'd come down here, spend all this time, go to all this trouble just to spy on you, to ferret out the *true* story of the strange double life of Jana Fitzgerald and Jay-Jay O'Dwyer? You really think your little secret is worth it?"

Jana fought the impulse to struggle, to try to evade his iron grip, to give him the satisfaction of resisting, without hope, his superior strength. "You came here," she said, tossing her hair from her eyes. "You knew who I was. You lied about knowing my father. You moved next door to me. You...you...practically tried to seduce me. You—"

"Stop it," he commanded, his hands around her wrists tightening. "Jana, you amaze me, you really do. You think I want your story? *Your* story?" he repeated, his voice cynical. "What story, Jana? 'Celebrity's Daughter Becomes Teacher'? Jana, just because you're hiding from life and love and memory and a dozen other things doesn't mean you have any story. You've made quite a respectable and ordinary life for yourself, and I wouldn't take it from you for the world. It's not worth the taking. It's not worth a paragraph in the tabloids. It's not worth anything to anyone but you."

Jana's stomach gave a sickening dip. A blackness rushed to cloud her head. Her knees weakened, and if Zack hadn't been holding her so tightly, she felt as if she might sag to the dead and frosty grass of the quad. What he said pierced her with a debilitating shaft of doubt—the righteousness of her moral outrage against him fled into the darkness, leaving her defenseless. "You could be lying," she said, her voice trembling.

"But I'm not."

Confusion swam through her. "How do I know that?"

He brought his face close to hers again, and for a moment the mercurial light played across his unsmiling face. "Because of what I told you. Your story's no story. If you asked all the students on this campus who Kevin O'Dwyer was, half wouldn't know. He's been dead too long. The other half might remember he was one of Tish Farrell's innumerable husbands. And none of them would remember you. It may sound cruel, Jay-Jay, but it's true. No story."

His use of her father's pet name for her stung. She fought the tears that pricked her eyes. Her own heart amazed her by telling her that she wished what Zack Devlin said was true and that he would go on holding her with no other motive than that he wished to hold her in his arms.

"So you see," he continued, his voice silken, scornful, "you made quite a scene tonight, and for no reason at all."

"I thought—" She stopped, her throat tight.

"No, you didn't think," he said harshly. "I don't mind being attacked. I'm rather used to it. I may never like it, but I'm used to it. But only in print or press conferences, not in university seminars and not by misguided women who forget they've sworn to uphold the best in journalistic inquiry."

"I didn't mean—"

"Whatever you meant to do—destroy me, whatever—hardly matters. What you did do was humiliate your department, which is a fine one, and Dr. Caxton, who is a kind and honorable man, and, of course, yourself. If you wanted to confront me, Jana, with a baseball bat or a revolver or whatever you deemed fit, all you had to do was walk into my office or my house and do it. But that wasn't good enough for you. You have some of your father's sense of the dramatic, I'll give you that, and all his fire and passion—I'll give you that as well. But your timing was nothing short of disastrous."

She tried to twist away from his accusations, but he held her fast.

"Don't struggle, Jana. You'll hear me out. You girded yourself up for a holy war, and like most people who go into a holy war, you became a fanatic, only for a night, but that was long enough to nearly hurt a number of people.''

Again she turned her face from him and stared at the towers, ghostly in the moonlight. She bit her lip. She had been so steeled by the rightness of her cause that she'd acted rashly, foolishly. But Zack would not make her cry. She swore that to herself.

"Did you see Dr. Caxton's face, Jana, when you launched your little onslaught?'' Zack sounded almost as if he enjoyed punishing her with his words. "He was mortified. You attacked his guest professor, along with his own credibility. You implied he was a fool to have me here. Not only that, but you violated some fundamental rules of your profession. I'm not a professor. I was a street-smart kid who got lucky. But I know that academics have a code of ethics. And that code says that a professor doesn't use a classroom situation to parade her own prejudices, especially not to try to humiliate someone else. She doesn't use a lecture as a forum for her own vindictiveness. She doesn't throw consideration for her department to the winds because she happens to dislike one member. She doesn't stoop to name-calling. Or mudslinging.''

"You're very moral all of a sudden,'' she said bitterly. "If I was that stupid, why did you even bother to save me?'' She gave the words a sardonic twist, but still could not meet his eyes.

"Perhaps I didn't do it for you at all,'' he said, a sneer in his voice. "Perhaps I did it for Caxton. Or the other faculty members. Or maybe I thought I still owed your father a little something, Jay-Jay. Maybe he wouldn't have wanted me to stand by and see his daughter make the biggest mistake of her career, then walk off and let her clean up the mess herself. So I cooked up a little deception to get you off the hook, not that you deserve it."

"And—" she turned to face him now, her voice sharp with suppressed tears "—I suppose I ought to thank you? Somehow you make that rather difficult. Is that what you want? My thanks? My apology? I don't feel like giving you either right now."

"I want only one thing from you," he said huskily. "I want you to walk back into that room as if nothing at all had happened tonight. Let them all wonder. It's for their sake as well as yours. Tomorrow you'll walk into your classrooms and tell your students to write an eyewitness account of what happened between us tonight. Tell them to be objective, pull no punches. You'll be surprised, I think, how much the idea will scare them. They'll be facing a scary journalistic situation—one they'll face in reality someday and that they'd better be prepared for. They won't know whether to try to please you or not. They won't know whether to take your side or not. They'll have to think for themselves. And they'll have to examine just how closely they observed what happened tonight, or if their own emotions and reactions got in the way. It may not be what you planned to do, but it won't hurt them a bit. And it ought to get you out of the hole you dug for yourself and the department."

"You're very inventive, Mr. Devlin," Jana said, fighting to keep her voice from trembling. "You're quite the knight in shining armor. Will you let go of me now?" She felt herself shuddering involuntarily, and a polar gust of night wind made her huddle closer to him.

"In a moment. Don't worry. I'll let you go before you turn into a real ice princess. But I have a few more things to say to you."

"Then say them!" Jana whispered miserably. "And let me go. I've had nothing but trouble since I met you, and I wish I never had...met you," she said with a little uneasiness.

"Oh, I'm sure you'll forget about me as soon as I leave Eastern," he gibed. "You're awfully good about blocking out things you don't want to think about. I think you acted like a little idiot tonight, Jana, and you nearly botched a number of things, including your own reputation. But in fairness I should tell you something else. Your past isn't all you're hiding from. It's your present and future as well. I said you hid from love..."

He stared down at her, his eyes unfathomable. Her heart hammered wildly in her throat, and for a moment she thought he was going to kiss her. Unconsciously she lifted her face to his. Her body softened in his arms, as if all that had happened tonight could somehow be made right again.

"But," he went on, "you've made it abundantly clear that love is something you want no part of. And that's no concern of mine. What is a concern is that you're also hiding from your talent. And in that matter, I have rights."

She did not know if it was the wind or something else that cut through her with such numbing coldness. "What do you mean?" she asked, her face still raised to his.

"I mean I've read some of the things you've written—your folder of tear sheets—and you can do with the written word what your father did with the spoken. Oh, you never write about anything of much consequence—that would take feeling—but your writing has a purity and an ardor that shines like burnished silver. It's something no one ever taught you and something you'll never be able to teach anyone else, no matter how good a teacher you are, because it's something that the gods gave you at birth—maybe to make up for all the sorrow you'd have to run from someday, I don't know.''

His voice and his grasp grew suddenly gentler, and for a few seconds he was silent, no longer looking down at her, but up at the glowing clouds that swept the moon. Then his tone turned harsh again. ''At any rate, you're doubly a fool if you don't use it,'' he said gruffly. ''Wasting your life is one thing. Wasting your talent is another. Don't do it.''

With every atom of her being, she fought the intoxication sweeping over her, the feelings welling inside her. ''I'm flattered,'' she said, the constriction in her voice sounding haughty. ''Now let go of me.''

''Oh, I'll let you go,'' he said caustically. ''And before long, I'll be out of your tidy little life forever. And I won't make you tremble in offense as you're doing now. I won't touch you anymore, Jana, as much as I might have liked to. If I ever *really* touched you, you might fall apart like one of those fragile little dolls you scatter around your house.''

Her thoughts, her senses, seemed to be flying out, blazing in all directions across the darkness, like the shooting flares of an exploding sky rocket, leaving her mind blinded, her body shuddering and unaccountably fevered in the night's cold vastness.

''Don't...don't...'' was all she could utter.

''Oh, don't worry, Jana,'' he mocked. ''I won't. And the odd thing is that I've wanted to, wanted to from the first time I saw you standing in front of me, looking like a sweaty little waif, a ragtag princess trying to outdistance a dragon. I saw all Kevin O'Dwyer's fire and fleetness, all the fine passion he once had born fresh and new again in you. I knew who you were before you ever opened your mouth. I wanted you, not your story, but you. That was before I knew how determined you were to create your own little world and dwell in it forever. What a misfortune, Jana. I can't help but think of what we both will miss."

He released her and reached one lean hand to straighten a lock of her dark hair. "Don't look up at me like that," he said, smiling down at her satirically, "with your eyes all dazzled and stricken. You proved in there tonight that you're a tough little fighter, even when you don't need to be. Shall we return? I'm sure most of them are in there wondering who's killed whom by now."

She took a step away from him, an unsteady step, feeling as if her knees would buckle under her, her high heels not support her weight.

"It's your chance now, Jana," he said, his tone bantering. "You may not like your father much, but you can draw on your legacy from him. You'll have to act a bit, and surely that's not beyond the power of Kevin O'Dwyer's daughter. We'll go back inside, pretend that we're neither friends nor foes, and nobody ever need know what really happened tonight. And we do have to go back in. I won't run away, and you can't. If you go flying off on my account one more time, people will think you're irrational. So you'll go back in there with me, and we'll let people think what they will. You'll pour your coffee and dispense your sugar and your smiles and your small talk. But don't worry. I'll stay out of your way after this. You can return to your doll-house in full safety, knowing that I'll leave you unmolested."

He tucked her unresisting arm into his and guided her back toward the library. Her stomach fluttered emptily, and her brain felt as if it had dissolved into a cloud of darkness.

He was right. She would have to go back in, make light of her attack on him. She would have to pretend for all concerned that they had planned the whole thing as a rather flamboyant experiment in teaching. She would have to be grateful to him for saving her from her own abysmal lack of judgment. She would have to pretend it had all meant nothing. She would stand there smiling, knowing all the time that she had been wrong, not just about Zack Devlin's intentions, but about the man himself. She was filled with a whirling sense of loss, a loss deeper than any she could remember since she had been a child, and another man had left her with nothing but shame and confusion too deep for her even to utter.

Somehow she got through the rest of the evening, even through Roger's suspicious looks and his remark that he hoped she *had* been kidding, because he thought she'd lost her marbles. She got through the next day and was amazed at how right Zack Devlin had been about her students. Three-quarters of them couldn't accurately describe what had taken place at all, and most of their accounts were muddled. Many looked worried when she told them to write, and not knowing if she would accept any critical remarks about herself, they chewed on their pencils in distress, casting furtive glances toward her desk.

After they had finished writing, Jana said, with a cold-bloodedness that surprised even her, that the whole scene had been a fabrication. She was shocked when a small contingent of students nodded wisely and said they'd known it all along.

"Ah, come on, Miss Fitzgerald," Brad, her best freshman student said, "I knew you couldn't mean it. You'd never do something like that. It wouldn't have been professional."

Jana thanked Brad curtly, then ducked her head to hide the blush that had leaped to her face.

Nell and Roger both said they'd had their students write on the incident and that the students learned a good deal about not only their own powers of observation, but about their objectivity. Zack Devlin didn't say anything. Only once or twice during the week that followed did he thrust his head through her office doorway and give her a chaffing smile. "Just to keep up appearances," he said, then withdrew.

They could not help but meet from time to time in the hall, and Jana felt her insides turn into a storm of butterflies each time she saw his tall figure approaching. Her smile always felt trembling, and Zack's always looked smugly false.

Sometimes she saw him from her kitchen window, playing with Sasha in the premature autumn cold, the pair chasing each other across the brown grass and tumbling in the heaps of maple leaves that he hadn't bothered to rake from the Babcocks' lawn. One weekend Christine was back with them, joining the rough-and-tumble, clad in form-fitting tan corduroys and a matching jacket with a sheepskin collar. Jana had turned away from the window that time, hurt in a way she did not understand by the carefree playfulness of the three of them.

The winds were sweeping out of the north and the west with precocious ferocity that fall, and already the trees were nearly bare, the skies a lifeless gray. Jana felt grimly that the season's mood matched her own, and her thoughts, when she allowed herself to think, were a subtle set of tortures.

Confict boiled within her, and she tried to cool it with the ice of logic. She could no longer deny that Zack Devlin attracted her, drew her with a powerful physical force almost primordial in intensity. Nor could she deny that the attraction both fascinated and distressed her. She had always thought herself immune to such yearnings, safely beyond them. Her father had been swept away on tides of feeling like this once, and nothing had been the same again. She'd sworn she'd never be pulled down by that same undertow of physical desire.

"It's physical," she told herself. "Only biology. A fluke of chemicals and glands. Something to be fought and overcome, like a craving for salt or alcohol."

But, her mind remonstrated, demanding equal time with itself, it's more than that. He'd saved her from herself that night she'd tried to assassinate his character at the lecture. He didn't have to do that. He didn't have to tell her he'd found her desirable. He didn't have to tell her she had talent she was wasting. He didn't have to do anything that night except turn his back and let her sink into the chaos she'd created herself.

Time out, a third part of her mind cried—the suspicious part that was strengthened by a reporter's training. Who said he had nothing to gain from helping her out of that mess? After all, she'd ended up reneging on all her charges, hadn't she, pretending she'd never meant a word of them? He was clever, and maybe he'd just outmaneuvered her again—not only outmaneuvered her, but guilefully steered her into a position where she almost had to be grateful. He might be trying to keep her off guard, bartering for her trust with false kindness, spurious compliments.

Order in the court! Jana's mind demanded. There's no sense in this! She could keep galloping around this squirrel wheel going nowhere for as long as she let herself. And that would lead only to frustration, madness, uncertainty, pain and the various other shocks the flesh was heir to. Better to forget him. She'd throw herself into her teaching. She'd run. She'd finally write that long letter to Les, not mentioning Zack Devlin at all.

She started running a new, longer route twice a day. Now she made the circuit between her house and the Coles County Fairground on the edge of town, that inauspicious stretch of land where Abraham Lincoln had once debated "the little giant," Senator Stephen Douglas. That had been one of the historic debates leading to Lincoln's ascent to the White House.

She revised all her old lesson plans and graded her papers more thoroughly than she needed to, filling the margins with red-inked advice. She wrote to Les with a warmth that would have surprised her a month and a half before. She even wrote a short article on the Amish community in Arthur, Illinois and sent it to the Sunday features editor of the travel-and-entertainment section of the *Chicago Tribune,* where she used to freelance while she was at grad school.

A week and a half later, when the wind was howling like an unlaid ghost around the window of her office, Jana's phone rang.

It was Stan Goble, the *Trib* editor. "Hello, gorgeous." he said.

"Stan! What's up? Did you get my article?"

"Love it, blue eyes, but tragedy strikes again. Just bought one on the Amish. Different slant. The one I just took is on their farming methods—you know, how they're still hitching old Dobbin to the plow and all that. Not as good as yours, but I don't want to run the pair too close together. Keep this and send it back to us next summer, okay? And hit that angle about their traditional clothing a little harder, okay? I know the women readers are going to want to know why these gals still consent to cloak themselves in bonnets and long skirts and wear no makeup."

"Consider it done," Jana said. "You want me to cut some of the material on the horse and buggy?"

"Naw," Stan said. "It's good stuff. But listen, dollface, that's not why I called. I can tell you all that in a letter and only be out postage. I got a hot proposition for you."

"An assignment, I hope," Jana said with a laugh. Stan always tried to sound lewd when he talked of propositions, but his thick Chicago accent always betrayed him.

"Yes, unfortunately an assignment, not a proposition," he sighed. "Look. Zack Devlin's been down there—what?—two months now. I'm surprised nobody's sent us anything. What say you do? A people piece. Nothing heavy. On spec, of course. You know—big-time J.-man among the cornfields, how the coeds drool, that sort of thing. Can you handle it?"

There was a beat of silence. "I don't think so, Stan," she finally answered. "Try somebody else. Roger, maybe. He could do you a good job. He and Devlin hit it off."

"Meaning you and Devlin didn't?" Stan returned. He was too good a newsman not to read between her words.

"Off the record," Jana said, "the most I'll say is 'no comment.'" She paused, unsure what to say next.

"Not to worry, cupcake," he said. "You may be better off staying away from him."

"What's that supposed to mean?"

"It means that if you were my daughter, which, alas and alack, you are young enough to be, I wouldn't send you near him. But since I'm just an old goat after a good story, I'd throw my ordinary compunction to the winds. You're not involved with him, are you?"

"No," she said, savoring the irony of it. "I'm not involved with him. Do you know him?"

"We've hoisted a few beers in our time."

"Do you think he's as good as they say?" Jana asked carefully, like someone venturing out onto cracked ice.

"As good and as bad," Stan said. "What's your impression?"

"Mixed," Jana said frankly. "That's why I'm asking you."

"He was the best before he got involved in all this heavy presidential biography stuff. Smart, original and ruthless."

Jana raised an eyebrow. "Honest?"

"As honest as anybody going after a story. But he takes chances. He can also charm the birds out of the trees, which helps."

"Professional ethics?"

"Let's just say this, sweetheart. If he can beat you out of a story, he will. And he'll make you think he's doing you a favor while he does it." A hint of bitterness had crept into Stan's guttural voice.

"On the line, Stan. Is Devlin a man to trust or not to trust?"

This time the pause was on Stan's end of the line. "A man to watch," he said. "Don't leave your diary lying around. Not that I dislike the guy—don't get me wrong."

Jana smiled to herself. Stan's words made everything easier. "Don't worry," she said. "Just wanted a professional opinion. Do you want me to buzz Roger's extension? He'd take the assignment."

"Yeah, sure, if he's around. And by the way, kid, got your snow boots out of the closet?"

"What?"

"Your snow boots, blue eyes. And your parka. Seen the latest long-range forecast?"

"I haven't seen anything except a pile of ungraded papers." Jana laughed.

"Got the winter of the century bearing down on us. Some fun, huh?"

"Weathermen are always wrong," Jana said. "I'll buzz Roger."

She pressed the button for Roger's office and for the first time in weeks felt a lightness within herself. Zack Devlin was a man to be watched, not trusted. Nobody to brood about. Nobody to care about. Nobody to concern her at all.

When she passed him in the hall that afternoon, and they exchanged artificial smiles, she felt the familiar drunken butterflies in her stomach. "Butterflies," she addressed them silently, "it's time to die. Winter's coming."

# CHAPTER SEVEN

WINTER CAME EARLY. Halloween night was not the usual tangy witches' brew of moonlight, rustling leaves, a hint of chill and a suggestion of smoke. It was a black bitter night with the sky alternately spitting snow and sleet, and the few trick-or-treaters who knocked at Jana's door were so bundled up she could hardly see their costumes.

On campus, the students streaming to and from class were swathed in jackets and mufflers, bent against the steady lash of wind that swept over the plains. Gone were the shorts and T-shirts of a few weeks before, and the tennis courts stood gray and deserted.

Still, no heavy snow had fallen, and people studied the sky in the time-honored manner of Midwesterners, who know that the weather has more tricks than any magician and some of those tricks are spectacular indeed. The classrooms were filled with students who sniffled, coughed, sneezed and went from class to class with boxes of tissues to staunch their streaming noses.

Jana indulged herself in a new blue-and-red running suit for winter, with a matching knitted cap. The campus, which had been full of runners in September, saw only the die-hard runners now, lonely figures who moved, heads down against the wind, their breath streaming behind them like smoke.

More often than not, Sasha still woke Jana in the morning. Why the other neighbors hadn't complained, Jana didn't know, unless they liked having a canine alarm clock set for 6:00 A.M. She would plod grumpily to the kitchen to put on her tea and would see the dog, prancing around on its chain, barking happily at the wind or perhaps at nothing at all.

Jana had developed a positive genius for avoiding Zack. She had a deep, inner tingling radar that seemed to tell her when he was in the halls, and when it began to vibrate she stayed in her office. If they had a faculty meeting, she sat as far as possible from him and in a place where their glances couldn't meet. She knew what time he left for classes in the morning and came home at night, and she timed her own departures and arrivals so she wouldn't see him. If she heard him in his yard shouting at Sasha as he threw the tattered Frisbee for her to fetch, she avoided the window, as if catching sight of him would turn her into stone.

She talked more about Les and continued to write him long letters. She was vaguely disappointed that when he wrote back, his letters were as cold and bloodless as ever. When Nell asked if she was counting the days until Les came home, Jana smiled with false brightness and said she certainly was.

She lied. She was counting the days until Zack Devlin left.

After the Thanksgiving break the semester would begin to wind down—a few more weeks of classes, then finals, and then he'd be gone. She told herself she couldn't wait. She told herself that she'd be glad. She still ran twice a day, and she took a lot of cold showers.

The day before Thanksgiving, the campus was empty. It was as if aliens from outer space had swooped down and kidnapped all the students. Except for a few foreign-exchange students, everyone had headed homeward for their turkey dinners and family gatherings. Nell, who had the instincts of a mother hen, always gathered up those few remaining students and invited them to her house to make sure that they got a taste of a "real American Thanksgiving dinner." She had them gorging on turkey, cranberry sauce, homemade rolls and pumpkin pie. She always worked herself to a frazzle and always loved it.

Thanksgiving had ceased to mean much to Jana. To think of families gathered around heaped tables disturbed her, reminding her of the family she'd lost. Although Roger usually succumbed to Nell's invitation and ended up eating turkey at her house, surrounded by students speaking in a dozen different languages, Jana always politely declined. She willed herself to make Thanksgiving into just another day, part of a long weekend she could use to catch up on grading papers.

Jana set out for her evening run to the fairgrounds and back, smiling to herself as she thought of Nell, who was probably fussing herself into a tizzy over preparations for the next day's feast. She would work herself to exhaustion, then Roger would scold her and spend the next two weeks grumbling that Nell might just as well have served hot dogs on paper plates—"What's all this foolishness about napkins and china and creamed peas, for God's sake?" he would say.

The sky was rapidly darkening and blue-black clouds hunched on the western horizon like a range of sinister mountains. The twilight air, although still, was thick with an unnatural duskiness. No wind blew, and the calm atmosphere offered no biting chill as Jana loped down the deserted streets toward the fairgrounds. Her blood pumped faster, her muscles loosened, and she began to feel warm, glad that her new running suit, which had been sinfully expensive, immediately absorbed perspiration and dispelled it to the outer air.

She had almost reached the fairgrounds when the first icy blast of wind hit her with such force that it nearly turned her around, but Jana kept running.

A moment later, a second assault of wind smashed into her like a wall of ice, hard enough to make her stumble. She stopped and looked up at the sky. The black western clouds were no longer a mountain, but an avalanche of darkness rolling across the sky. Even as she stood watching the clouds streaming in like a mass of witches, she felt the temperature drop.

Immediately she turned and headed home, hoping to beat the blizzard. She had been a Midwesterner long enough to know that snowstorms were neither cozy nor romantic. On the plains, weather was king, and a tyrannical one, capricious and cruel. She cursed herself for not having checked the weather report before she left.

She'd run a little more than a block when the storm hit—as suddenly as the strike of a snake. The sky blackened, the wind knocked into her, and the air was suddenly swarming with white needles of snow. The running suit that was almost too warm a few moments ago now seemed to offer as much protection against the cold as netting.

Gales of wind buffeted her, and somewhere into the dimness she heard the rumbling clang of trashcans blown over and rolling before the tide of wind. The snow whirled around her like a thousand tiny ghosts trying to shut her eyes, sting her face. The air suddenly seemed too cold to breathe; each gulp she took burned her aching lungs.

She pushed herself for speed, trying to wipe the snow from her eyes. The flakes felt more like slivers of cold steel than snow, and she marveled how, on the plains, the wind rushed with such force that it seemed to slam into her sideways, as if it didn't really wish to fall at all, but was stampeding toward Indiana.

*Come on*, she said to herself. *This is really sort of exhilarating, plunging through the cold and the biting whiteness that rends the gathering dark. It's sort of like a do-it-yourself sauna,* she rationalized. *First you work up a sweat, then you fly through the snow.*

But she wished she could see better and that the slashing wind didn't pierce her like a sword of ice. She indulged herself in a brief thought of a hot shower and a cup of warm mulled cider, then gave her mind back to running.

With less than a mile to go, almost halfway home, she felt the familiar stitch in her side, and her lungs felt choked and frozen. It was then she felt her heel come down wrong on the cement, and before she even had time to cry out, she was on the ground, holding her knee in pain, the snow whipping down on her.

Even though her mind went blinding white with the flash of pain, she knew what she'd done: she had locked her knee and stretched the tendon. Tears bit at her eyes as she gripped both hands around the injured knee and writhed on the snowy ground.

She lay for a moment in misery, bitterly cold, agony knifing up and down her leg, the snow slicing at her. *The snow,* she thought. *Get up,* she thought. *Get home.*

She tried to rise, but the wind slapped her down, and she cried with pain as she fell on her injured knee.

Doggedly she rose again, setting her jaw. She hunched over, both hands still bracing the knee, and began to hobble forward.

The air was black now, the snow thicker and sharper. She almost bumped into a tree, then realized she had better keep to the edge of the street with the curb to guide her. Visibility was extremely limited.

Each step was torture, her progress maddeningly slow. She tried to think of nothing except her next step, but her mind churned up memories of horror stories about people in blizzards—the farmer lost between his house and the barn, the school children who never found their way home. *No, no,* she thought, willing herself onward. *That was a century ago—the great prairie storms. Don't be melodramatic. All that happened in pioneer days, on the open prairie. Nobody froze to death in the middle of a town.*

She limped on, head down, gritting her teeth. She no longer had any feeling in her fingers, and her feet didn't seem to belong to her. How much farther did she have? Five blocks? Four?

She could stop, she could ask for help, but all she wanted to do was to get home. Besides, she thought dully, there was nobody home, not a light to be seen. Everyone had gone away for Thanksgiving. Over the river and through the woods, to grandmother's house they go…leaving their dark houses empty behind them.

She could not remember ever being so cold. The cold jabbed into her very marrow, crowding out all warmth and feeling. The cold was everywhere, infinite and piercing. The cold was exactly her size. She was the cold. Suddenly she wanted nothing more than to lie down and sleep. If she could sleep for a moment, she could make it the rest of the way.

*No,* she thought, shaking her head. If she went to sleep, she could freeze to death. Another horror story crept into her mind—only two years ago, the man in the stalled car who'd tried to fight his way across a field through the storm to a deserted house for shelter. He'd never made it.

She wished a light shone somewhere. She wished somebody was home. All these houses and nobody home. Nobody to help. But she only had a block to go. *Not much farther,* she thought. *Only forever.*

Then another monster gust of wind tore at her and she went down again. She would have wept with frustration, but she was too tired. Only a block to go. Her knee hardly hurt now; she could barely feel it, but she couldn't make it move, either. She could probably move it if she lay there, just a moment. If she slept just a tiny while she could move again. And then she'd be home. She sank into cold darkness.

Somebody was trying to wake her. Somebody was pelting her face with warm plums, and she could smell something hot and vaguely unpleasant. Somebody was trying to shake her hand, steal her knitted cap, lick her face. She wanted only to sleep, to rest.

Warm plums poking at her face again, and a noise like a whine. How ridiculous, she thought—that's a dog's nose that keeps bumping me, a big, warm, wet dog's nose, and a dog's hot, meaty breath. *Go away, you stupid dog, and let me sleep.*

Then there was a light that hurt her eyes, so she closed them again, and strong arms hoisting her up and carrying her somewhere—her father maybe. Her father was putting her to bed, and she was glad because she was so tired.

Suddenly the wind was gone, and the dog was licking her face again, trying to wake her. Then rough hands were on her, shaking her and pushing something to her mouth.

"Drink this!" The voice sounded strangely familiar. She liked it. She wondered why everything was so dark. She saw a fire dancing in the corner, but it hurt her eyes, and she tried to close them again.

"I said, drink!" the voice ordered. "Down, Sash. Let her alone. Good girl."

There was a glass at her lips and obediently she sipped at it, then choked. Somebody beat her on the back, and made her drink again. She did, choked again, and tears burned her eyes.

"Keep drinking. Let me get those shoes and your gloves off," he said. He seemed to take off her shoes and gloves, but perhaps he only pretended to, because she couldn't feel anything. She watched him dumbly, not helping him. She suddenly realized she was cold and began to shudder.

"That's good, that's good," he said. "Take another drink." She obeyed him, and he was rubbing her hands so hard she could almost feel them. He wrapped a blanket around her and picked her up, setting her down close to the orange fire. The fire felt funny to her. It felt warm. It hurt. The warmth made her itch and tingle. The dog was licking her face again. It felt good.

The man was gone a long time and then he returned with a tea kettle. Perhaps they were going to have tea. No, instead he poured some warm water into a basin and made her put her feet in it. It hurt. He rubbed her hands some more. She could feel now, and it hurt, as if her fingers were full of sharp sparkles. Then he clamped her hands between the warmth of his thighs so tightly she could feel the ridged seams of his denims, and he made her drink another glass of stuff that burned her throat. He was a very handsome man, and she thought she knew him well.

"I was a Boy Scout," he rumbled at her, as she grimaced from the drink, "but in California. I think you'll live, but I won't guarantee it. All the first aid I had consisted of treating surfboard injuries. I always dreamed of giving mouth-to-mouth resuscitation to a beautiful blonde in a bikini, but I guess you'll have to do."

She looked at him, her eyes narrowing with suspicion.

"Are you coming to?" he asked. "If you are, don't say something corny like 'What happened?' I've got that question reserved for myself. And sooner or later you're going to have to get out of those clothes. I'd take you out of them myself, but the way we've been hitting it off, you'd have me in Joliet Prison for attempted rape. So you're going to have to undress yourself. Think you can do it?"

She nodded numbly and watched him take her hands from between his warm thighs, rub them again, then rise and leave the room. Firelight flickered on the walls, and she wondered why the room was so dark. She shook her head to clear it. The dog at her feet gave her a happy whine and a thump of its tail. Jana realized, with a slow blooming of wonder, that she was in Zack Devlin's house and that she hurt all over and that her teeth were chattering and her body was shuddering convulsively.

# CHAPTER EIGHT

ZACK RETURNED and laid a bundle of clothing in front of the fire. "You'll have to make do with that," he said, turning to look down at her. He was silhouetted by the firelight. "Nothing so cute and hokey as my pajamas, though I did give you my robe. Dress in front of the fire. It's warmest there."

He knelt before her and with surprising gentleness took her feet from the water and dried them with a thick towel. "I don't think you're frostbitten," he said. "At least there's no discoloration. I'm going to leave the room. Get dressed."

She stood up shakily and limped toward the fire. Pain shot through her injured knee, and her fingers felt thick and clumsy. It took a long time to shed the damp running suit, her panties and jogging bra. Zack's choice of garments for her was decidedly helter-skelter—a large thermal undershirt that hung almost to her knees, a worn pair of boy's jeans, probably left behind by one of the Babcock's sons, a boy's faded flannel shirt, two pairs of woolen socks, and a man's bathrobe. Her awkward fingers trembled and she fumbled with the buttons and snaps. She could not stop shaking.

"How are you doing?" His voice came from the darkness.

"I—I can't button the buttons," she chattered. "I'm too cold."

He padded in and stood before her in front of the fire. "Worse than having a kid," he grumbled, snapping the jeans for her. He buttoned the shirt up to her neck, then bundled her into the heavy robe. "Can you get the socks on? Or do I have to do that, too?"

"I—I think so," she said, feeling weak. "Let me sit down." She hobbled back to the chair and sat. Her hands shook but she got on both pairs of stockings.

"What's wrong with your leg?" he asked gruffly.

She wrapped her arms around herself, trying to get warm. "I took a wrong step. About a mile from home. I h-hurt it. My knee. An overextension, I think they call it. P-pulled tendon. You feel like your knee is b-bending backward."

"Let me see." He was on his knee by her side again, rolling up the leg of the faded jeans. "You're swollen. Looks like somebody implanted a baseball. Let me check out the old medicine cabinet, kid. And stop shaking. I don't want to give you any more brandy. You'll get drunk."

She sat, clutching the robe tightly around herself. She remembered the fall and the long, torturous creeping through the snow, but she couldn't remember how or when it had ended, or how she had arrived in Zack Devlin's living room.

He was beside her again, wrapping an athletic bandage around her knees. His powerful hands were surprisingly deft, and she watched the firelight glitter on his black hair.

"Better?" he asked, looking up at her. The firelight played across his features.

"I guess."

"Give me those hands. You're still frozen." He took her hands and blew on them, then rubbed them between his own. "Tell Uncle Zack what happened. How did you manage to be out in that bloody blizzard? I nearly froze my buns off coming to your rescue. It's kind of cold out there."

"I t-told you. I was running. The storm hit. I pulled something, but I tried to get home. I was going home. Then I don't know what happened."

He continued to rub and blow on her hands.

"Well, my dear," he said, giving one of her palms a hot kiss, then the other, "you overshot the mark. You went right past your house. Mine, too, in fact. You were headed straight for the highway, and from there, who knows? The cornfields, perhaps, where they would have found your little body next spring, as blue as a turquoise and twice as stiff. You're lucky I was around. Or maybe you'd have rather frozen to death than have to be grateful to me, eh?" He smiled up at her sardonically.

She felt foolish and defenseless. "What were you doing?" she shot back. "Just wandering around with your flashlight, like Diogenes, looking for people to save?"

He raised his eyebrows in mock surprise. "Oops! It's coming back to life. It can hurl insults again. Is it thankful to me? Of course not."

"Look," Jana said, still shaking, "I'm glad you found me. I just wondered how, that's all. I mean, of course, I'm grateful, but I think I'd just sort of lain down a minute to rest..."

"Of course," he said. "With your head in a snow-drift and your feet in the street. I always rest that way myself. Actually, I had nothing to do with finding you. You could have frozen on my very doorstep, and I'd have sat in here with my fire and my brandy, none the wiser. It was Sash who knew something was out there. Her ears went up, her tail went down, she got a look of consternation in those beautiful eyes. The Russians are mystical, you know. And they have a thing for snow. She wanted out and I let her out. Sash thinks God invented snowstorms solely for her amusement."

He squeezed her fingers, stroked her wrists. "She went out. She found you. I wasn't going out, I assure you—I have more sense. But she'd run back to me and bark, then run off into the darkness again, then back to me. It was wonderful. Just like a Lassie movie. Only much more dramatic. Sash has a flair for drama, you know. The way she carried on, I thought she'd found a unicorn at least. When I finally followed her, she was pulling on you, trying to wake you up or drag you. Oh, you should have seen it—so heartwarming that I nearly wept. Of course, she may have just been trying to decide if you were already dead so she could bury you like a bone or eat you like some peasant who'd been thrown off his cart."

His attitude struck her as cruelly cavalier. "You mean," she grumbled, "I was saved by that dopey dog? I have to be grateful to her for the rest of my life?"

"Precisely." He grinned, looking a little wolfish himself in the firelight. "Send her Christmas cards for the rest of her days. Buy her sirloin tips on Valentine's Day. Remember her in your will. All of it. You might be grateful to me, too. I was the one who went wading out and carried you back in here, and shared my fire, and gave you my second-best brandy and buttoned your buttons for you. But don't worry about Christmas cards. I'll think of some other way for you to thank me."

Again he kissed the palm of each of her hands. He raised her fingers, pressed them to his lips and blew against them. His mustache made her fingertips tingle.

"I—I think I should go home now," she said uneasily.

He breathed on the fingers of her other hand. "And I think not," he said. "I think you should stay here."

Jana felt the old familiar butterflies, but this time they were swarming in her head as well as her midsection. "I want to go home now," she said, her voice trembling. "I want to go home and take a shower and crawl under my electric blanket."

"You can't," he said, kissing the inside of her wrist, where a blue vein leaped wildly.

"But I want to," she said, feeling like a tired child ready to cry from exhaustion.

"You can't, my darling popsicle," he murmured, kissing the inside of her other wrist. "Hmmm," he said. "I do believe you're warming up. No, Jana, you can't go home. The electricity is off, in case you haven't noticed. The lines must have gone down almost as soon as the storm hit. So even if I took you home, you'd have no nice shower, because there's no hot water and no electric blanket, for obvious reasons."

"I still want to go home," she said. She tried to pull her hands away from him, but he held them fast. "I want to go home."

"Do you have a fireplace?" he asked, one eyebrow cocked.

"No."

"Do you have a gas oven?"

"No..."

"Jana, you're still nearly frozen. I'm not taking you back there. Great Scott, if it's like the Arctic in here, even with the fire, what'll your place be like? You're in no shape to camp out. Stay here and sleep by the fire. The Babcock kids have sleeping bags. By tomorrow the lines will be repaired and I'll take you home. I know you don't like me, but—''

For the first time, Jana felt too exhausted to cope any further. She ducked her head and felt a tear slide down her face. ''I'm so stupid!'' she said.

His hands on hers were suddenly still. She could feel his eyes on her.

''What do you mean?'' His voice was suddenly husky.

''I could have stopped,'' Jana said, choked. ''I went on, like a fool, trying to make it home, because I thought all the houses were empty. They were just dark because the electricity was out. How stupid!''

''Oh,'' he said. He started rubbing her hands, more roughly now. ''There,'' he said, letting go of her. ''I think you'll live to play piano again. Do link puzzles. Repair watches. And stop sniveling. I hate women with runny noses. I'll go get your sleeping bag.''

He rose and disappeared into the darkness, and Jana slumped over, burying her face in her hands. She still felt cold and helpless and confused.

She supposed she'd been in some kind of shock, too cold and scared to think clearly. Anybody might have made such a mistake and blundered on through the storm. But now she was sitting in Zack Devlin's house, in front of his fire, and he was making her feel the same strange and vulnerable way again, and she just didn't feel strong enough at the moment to fight it all any longer. Her flesh prickled and stung, trying to come back to life, but more painful was the unwanted desire that swept over her in his presence. Her knee throbbed, a constant reminder of what a mess she'd let her life become.

She heard him enter and looked up. He stood tall in the doorway, the sleeping bags under his arm, and a narrow mattress balanced on one broad shoulder.

"One of the Babcock kids' bunk-bed mattresses," he said roughly, and let it fall by the fire. "You'll be warmer over here. I'll take the couch. As for the sleeping bags—which would you rather have—the one with Smurfs on it or the one with Superman?"

At the sound of his voice, she started to cry harder. She put her face in her hands again. "Smurfs!" she sobbed.

She heard him spreading the sleeping bag, then felt him bending over her. "Come on," he said, taking her in his arms and lifting her from the chair. "Upsy-daisy. You've had a long night. Stop crying. Stop crying. My God, you're still shaking. Stop it. Come on. Stop it."

His mustache was nuzzling her ear, and her arms went around his neck. She buried her face against his shoulder, the tears flowing hotly.

He set her down on the opened sleeping bag, but she still clung to him, crying.

"Jana," he said in her ear. "It's all right. It's all over now. Everything's fine. Sleep, baby. You need sleep. Rest. Don't cry, sweetheart. Don't."

He drew her face from his shoulder and held it between his hands. "Don't," he said, and kissed the tears.

Then he lowered his mouth to hers, and the fierce tenderness of his kiss made her shudder throughout her body. Her arms circled his neck more desperately. She felt the firmness of his lips upon her own, the flick of his tongue as he gently forced her lips to part and let the hot sweetness of his tongue enter, searching hungrily.

His arms were around her, his strong hands pressing her waist and back to mold her against his hard body. He kissed her cheeks, her eyelids, her brows, her temples, then took her lips again, possessing them and her body and all the emotions she felt straining within her, straining to join him, to become one with him. She shuddered again, and he raised his mouth from hers, staring down into her hazy eyes.

"Jana," he whispered hoarsely. "Are you still cold?"

She looked up into the hazel eyes with their dark lashes, their strong dark brows. She tried to smile. She nodded. "I feel like I've been cold forever," she said, her voice broken. "I feel like I'll never be warm again."

He ran the back of his fingers across her cheekbone.

"Would you like me to warm you?" he asked, his other hand tangling in the curls at the back of her neck.

Again she nodded, feeling all her emotions breaking free like a spring river against the last of winter's ice and flowing, lively and ready, to him.

"Then let me," he whispered against her throat. "Let me."

Again he found her lips, his tongue softly delving the secrets of her mouth. He kissed her with a passion that was surging, molten. His sinewy hands possessed the contours of her arching back, her ribs, her throat. She felt his mustache graze the line of her jaw, his tongue taste the hollow of her throat.

Still his mouth drank hers. He unbuttoned the buttons he'd fastened before, and his warm hand was under her clothing, stroking the satiny skin of her breast, filling her with turmoil. She was exhilarated as she felt him lift the shirt and cup both her breasts in his fervid hands, felt his loins press against her own. Each touch whetted her hunger for more. The depth of her desire frightened and intoxicated her. She drew back from him for a moment, weak.

Then he was leaning above her, staring down at her face in the flickering light on the fire. He was breathing hard, his face strained. "Jana." His voice was ragged. "I want you. All of you. I want to know and make love to every part of you. I want to touch you and taste you and explore you, as if you were a delicate little continent of pleasures that was mine alone. Do you understand me?"

Dazed, drugged by his kisses, she looked up at him. How can this be happening, she thought. Is this how it happens? What happens then, after? Unconsciously she put her arm across her breasts to cover them.

"I want you," he repeated, voice taut. "But... perhaps this isn't the time. Or the place. Or the circumstances. I'd wake up tomorrow wondering if it was the storm. Or the brandy. Or exhaustion. And so would you. You know that, don't you?"

His eyes swept over her, and she crossed both arms over her breasts, as if to protect herself from his demanding eyes. Her lips quivered.

He laid a finger on them. "You're tired, Jana. And scared and confused. I'm not sure you really want me. You may just want human warmth. That's fine, because sometimes we all need it. But I want more than that from you. The old look is already creeping back into your eyes, your face. I don't think you even know it's there most of the time."

Suddenly she felt empty, weary, ashamed. She turned her face away from him, her hair fanning out against the flannel of the sleeping bag. The real world came crowding back on her, and she wondered tiredly at her own stupidity.

"That look you wear, Jana," he said, his voice half scoffing, the way it usually was, "is terror. Pure terror shines out of those blue eyes. Always terror. All your defenses are beaten down tonight. Tomorrow it may be different. I don't want you, as they so quaintly say, 'to hate yourself in the morning.'" He raked a hand through his dark hair. "I don't want to see you looking any more haunted than you do. You won't even meet my eyes now, will you?"

She stared into the fire, watching it leap and flicker. She would not look at him. "Sex I can always get, Jana. Quite good sex, too. Without complications. But for you, it's different. It would be different."

He was silent for a long time. He gave her hip a brotherly pat. "Besides," he said, a laugh in his voice, "I can't throw you out into a snowbank every time I want to make love to you. That's taking foreplay to new extremes."

She stared at the flames.

"Go to sleep, Jana," he said. He kissed her temple. "I'll keep you warm. Don't worry." He lay down beside her, pulling the flap of the sleeping bag over her, wrapping his strong arms around her. She felt his warmth through the length of her body, but he touched her no further.

Outside the wind howled like a demented thing. There was a rustle as Sasha rose from her rug and came to lower herself at the foot of the sleeping bag, resting her head on Jana's foot.

Jana leaned back against Zack's muscled warmth. She felt lost and safe at the same time. But she was warm at last. She slept.

# CHAPTER NINE

SHE AWOKE to the tantalizing smell of bacon frying, but when she tried to stretch, an involuntary yip of pain escaped her. Every part of her body seemed to hurt. With a start she realized where she was, and memories of the night before came swarming back. She wanted to burrow deeper into the sleeping bag and never come out, but her cry had brought Sasha, tail wagging, to her side, and the dog's face was thrust into hers, the crazy yellow eyes smiling. Sasha gave her face a slobbery lick, and Jana yipped again.

"Rise and shine," said Zack. "I have a clear case of role reversal on my hands, doing woman's work while you lie abed, and I don't like it." He was crouched before the fire, holding a skillet over the flames. He wore jeans, a heavy cable-knit sweater and a plaid wool jacket.

He seemed unfazed by the previous night, and she decided she should follow suit. "Call off your dog," she said, watching Sasha hunker beside the sleeping bag and begin chewing on its corner.

"You slept twelve hours," he said. "Not bad. World class, I'd say. If there were a sleeping Olympics, you'd bring home the gold. You snore, you know."

"I do not," Jana said indignantly and tried to pull the sleeping bag from Sasha's grip.

"How do you know?" he asked. He set down the skillet and moved over beside her, sitting next to the dog. "Don't, Sash. It's impolite to eat the guest's bed. No, I lied. You don't snore. You sigh a lot, but no snoring."

He leaned down and gave her a brief kiss that caught her by surprise. "How do you feel?"

She smiled. "Sore."

"To be expected. No electricity yet, as you can see. And if we're going to eat, I'd better tend to the bacon. Go clean up—it should be ready by then. It's going to have to be instant coffee, I'm afraid." He nodded at a pot of water sitting in the coals.

Jana crawled from the sleeping bag and groaned again. Her knee hurt and seemed opposed to bending. She hobbled down the hall, clutching Zack's large robe around herself. The bathroom was so cold she could see her breath. She washed her face and hands in icy water and found a box in the medicine cabinet with a new toothbrush in it. She brushed her tangled hair with one of Zack's brushes.

Her reflection stared back at her, remarkably clear-eyed. She looked a bit pale, but no worse for wear. He had kissed her good morning. She didn't know what that meant, but she liked it. She stretched luxuriously, feeling her muscles limbering. She felt oddly light-hearted, as if she might be snowed in forever and what happened here was not related in any way to the world outside.

The bathroom window was frosted over with a thick veil of ice and ice flowers, and she could hear the wind outside, still shrieking, although its note was lower now.

She made her way back to the living room and lowered herself beside Zack at the fireplace. He was filling two plates with strips of crisp bacon and scrambled eggs. Two mugs of coffee steamed beside the plates.

"I've got good news and bad news," he said, handing her a plate. "First the good news. The storm's nearly over. I braved it out to the car and listened to the radio this morning. The bad news is there's another one right behind it, sweeping in from the Rockies. We're talking record-breaking snows. They haven't been able to get out the repair crews yet. Don't know when we'll have heat again. And a bunch of phones knocked out. We may be here awhile." He clinked his coffee mug against hers. "So happy Thanksgiving, neighbor, and if you're wondering what the feast will be, the answer is canned chili."

She sipped her coffee and watched him over the top of her cup, feeling suddenly shy. He hadn't shaved this morning, and his jaw was dark with stubble. She wanted to reach out and run her fingertips over it.

Sasha lay at their feet, watching each bit of food they took. Her tail thumped mournfully.

Zack finished his coffee and wiped his hand across his mustache. A wry look glittered in his golden eyes. "You know," he said, "you're very quiet this morning. I don't know what to make of it. When you're not insulting me, I don't quite know what to do with you. I hope you're not suffering any morning-after compunctions, especially since you didn't do anything."

In spite of the chill, a slow burning invaded her cheeks. "I don't usually..." She poked a fragment of egg with her fork and blushed more deeply, remembering the scene on the sleeping bag. "I don't usually... cry," she finished lamely.

He reached over and straightened the collar of the large bathrobe. "Last night was not a usual night," he said easily, "for either of us, I would imagine. I'm not usually so noble. I'm the one who hates himself this morning. Or at least is kicking himself. You really looked quite fetching, abandoning yourself to passion on a bag covered with Smurfs."

"It wasn't you," she said between her teeth. "It was the Smurfs. They happen to turn me on."

He seized her arm and stared down into her eyes. "You, too? Jana, I didn't know how to tell you this, but it was the same for me. It wasn't you—it was the Smurfs! Perhaps we can have a relationship after all."

She laughed, and he took the plate from her lap, set it on the hearth, bent down and kissed her. The stubble of his beard was rough against her face, but the scrape against her skin filled her with happiness. His long arms circled her, pulling her against his chest. He kissed her so deeply she was dizzied, then he drew back and stared down into her eyes.

"So we're friends?" he asked, tracing her eyebrow with his thumb. "Maybe even good friends?"

She smiled and put her forefinger on his mustache. "Friends. Maybe even good friends." She smiled.

He lowered his face to hers again, but a gentle slup-slupping sound made them both turn. Sasha, eyes wary, was lapping up the last of Jana's breakfast.

"Sash!" Zack shouted. He lunged for a sofa pillow and flung it at the dog, who dodged it and fled for the farther regions of the house.

Jana laughed, and Zack jumped up and flew after the dog. From a back room came sounds of a scuffle and a yelp of remorse.

He came back dragging the dog behind him. Sasha's ears were laid back, her eyes wild with the knowledge that she was once again in trouble. Jana, weak with laughter, leaned against the bricks of the fireplace.

"Down!" Zack thundered, and the dog sank to its rug, a portrait of penitence. Zack flopped down beside Jana and put his arms around her shoulders.

"Why do you have that impossible creature?" she asked, leaning against his chest.

"She was guaranteed to drag nubile maidens out of snowstorms," he said. "And I like her. We're two of a kind."

"What kind?" Jana asked. "Both lone wolves?" In her heart, she feared that's what Zack was and always would be.

"No," he said, his voice suddenly serious. "Two crossbreeds. Two wild cards that don't quite fit into the scheme of things. My friend—he's half Inuit, lives in Anchorage—got her mother. God knows how. A beautiful thing. Pure Siberian timber wolf. Moved like a shadow, like the wind. He was using her to crossbreed with huskies, trying to get a tougher sled dog. But Sasha's mother had ideas of her own. Made a love match with a German shepherd. Mostly the pups looked like her, and people wanted them. Except this one. She had one lop ear and looked exactly like what she was— a mongrel. She broke my heart. She was half wild and half tame, and she loved people. I swear she needed them—maybe needed them to perform her life's work, which is driving human beings nuts. But I took one look at those crazy yellow eyes, and I said, 'Baby, you've got a home.' I can't tell you how many fine hotels she's got me kicked out of. The list is impressive. Really."

"So how are you alike?" Jana asked, wishing he would say that he, too, needed somebody.

"Crossbreeds," he said. "I never knew who my old man was. I assume it was a love match. My mother was young, a kid really. She finally married somebody else. You know Chino, California? You remember that place?"

Jana nodded. She remembered vaguely, from her Hollywood days.

"Chino's where we ended up. My stepfather's business was liquor stores. He robbed them. Unfortunately his business failed, and he wound up in Chino. It's a prison town. My mother moved us there so she could visit him. She worked as a hotel maid."

He took Jana's hand in his, and his thumb stroked her palm. "I thought I had it tough being a poor little rich girl," she said, studying their linked hands.

"I really need violin accompaniment for this sad story," Zack said. His voice was mocking, but for the first time she began to sense the complexities his mockery hid. "I hated my stepfather, so I tried to follow in his footsteps. I guess I thought that would be a sort of punishment for him. When I was fourteen that made more sense to me than it does today," he said. "I was always in trouble, but I thought I was quite a guy. And there was nobody who could control me. I got in fights and was into petty thievery."

He paused. "I'll tell you, Jana, but I don't talk about it much. The next part is something you may not like to hear. But you deserve to know. If you hate me for telling you, that's my loss."

She looked up at him, her heart beating hard. She could no longer imagine hating him. She wanted this day to go on forever, the two of them sitting by the fire, she nestled against his lean body.

"I was a fairly accomplished thief. Stripping cars was my specialty. I could get four hubcaps in sixty seconds flat. I also proved adept at breaking into cars. The only advantage of my misspent youth is that I'll never be locked out of anything. I could probably jimmie open a bank vault. One night, around midnight, I was walking past a bar, a real dive, when I saw the car of my dreams. A white Cadillac, about two blocks long, with the back seat full of stuff—a leather jacket, I remember that—and some other things—and there was no way I could resist. My key to magic worlds was a bent coat hanger I always carried around. I whipped it out, slid it through the top of the window and popped the lock button up. With my coat hanger, I was Ali Baba—open, Sesame. I was looting merrily, when a pair of hands grabbed me from behind and turned me around and threw me against the side of that Caddy so hard that it knocked the wind out of me. He wasn't a tall guy, but he had shoulders like an ox. I was taller than he was, but still just a lanky kid, and I had that sinking sensation you get when you know you've just offended a guy capable of killing you. 'You'll end in a bloody borstal,' he says, 'The devil take you for his own.' He also said a number of other colorful things I won't repeat to you. He was half-drunk, and when he drank, I later learned, the Irish brogue always came back. It was your father, Jana."

For some reason, this time mention of her father didn't make her flinch. The Tish Farrell affair suddenly seemed a long time ago. Zack looked down at her. "This is the part you may not like," he said. "Do you want me to go on?"

She traced her finger across the dark stubble of his cheek. "Yes," she whispered.

"Okay. The upshot of it was that he held me there until the cops came, and I kept thinking, 'This is crazy. He's a drunken Irishman who only comes up to my shoulder.' But there was a certain terrible intensity in him that made me wonder just what kind of demon I'd uncorked. When the police turned me around to frisk me, they found a book in my hip pocket. A paperback copy of *The Shropshire Lad*. I'd stolen it from somewhere a long time before, and I always carried it around. I liked it without even knowing why. He saw it and he said, 'Do you read this?' and I made some smart answer. But he said, 'If you've read it, boy, say me a poem.' So there I stood, spread-eagled against his Cadillac, and I recited, With Rue My Heart Is Laden. He said 'T'is no ordinary thief you are, but François Villon'—not that I'd ever heard of François Villon, at that point.

"The upshot of it all was that he started reciting poetry there, out on the sidewalk in that great big glorious voice, and telling the police to take their hands off me, that I was a fine broth of a boy. We ended up in the back of the same police car, him for drunk and disorderly conduct. He recited Shakespeare all the way to the station.

"He phoned Tish and she sent somebody to bail him out, and he insisted they put up bail for me too. And he refused to press charges. Which was lucky for me, because one more arrest and I'd have been in reform school.

"He and Tish were in Chino making a film, one of the really bad ones—the one about the corrupt prison warden. I ended up getting driven home in the back of a Rolls-Royce, and the man was still reciting poetry. He said they were going to be there six more weeks, to come and see him, that he had a son himself. And I did go to see him. That's how it started."

"He had a wonderful voice, didn't he?" Jana asked, her throat tight. She remembered Kevin O'Dwyer leaping wildly about the living room, reciting the bloodier passages of *Hamlet*, brandishing a rolled-up newspaper as a sword, while she and her brother squealed with delight. She remembered him by her bedside, reading *The Three Bears* to her in that wonderful voice that made each bear come alive, as distinct and real as her father himself.

"He made me love words," Zack said, pulling her closer. "He got me drunk on words. He taught me a lot in six weeks. I'd never met anybody like him. He never talked down to me. But he made me promise to stop stealing hubcaps and to finish school. He convinced me I could be somebody."

She looked up at him, trying to imagine him at fourteen, how her father had seen him that night, and those days following. She knew he had seen her father as she had when she was a little girl—a man larger than life, radiating magic.

"Does hearing all this bother you?" he asked, his brow furrowed.

She shook her head. "No. It's funny, but it doesn't. He was something, wasn't he?"

Zack grinned. "That he was. We kept in touch over the next few years. I was surprised he had time to write to me, but at that age my ego was big enough that I thought I was a pretty amazing guy. I didn't realize then just how extraordinary it was. Once when things got tough, I even hitchhiked to Beverly Hills to talk to him, and we stayed up half the night figuring out the world. Tish didn't like it. She always looked at me as if I was casing the place so I could make off with the silverware. I didn't like her much, either. She wore so much makeup I always wondered why it didn't make her pitch forward."

He rose and put another log on the fire. "I couldn't afford college. Even with a scholarship. But Kevin came through again. He called up an old drinking buddy from the *L.A. Times*. I started stringing stories in to them. Kevin even fed me a couple on him and Tish. She didn't like that, either."

He stoked the fire and stared into it pensively. "He wasn't a well man, even then. Things had started to go wrong for him, and he had been hitting the bottle harder than ever. He was in terrible shape near the end. A lot of people didn't want anything more to do with him, but I never felt that way. To me, he was the genie who showed me the magic door out of Chino. He taught me a lot. About more than words. And he did love you, Jana. You and your brother both. Losing the two of you haunted him, and he never really got over it."

She put her arms around her knees and bent her head to rest her face against them. "I always loved him, too," she said. "It was just so hard to admit. When he left, it was like the stars all fell from the sky. But I always loved him."

He knelt beside her and took her in his arms. "Beautiful blue-eyed Jay-Jay, the prettiest colleen in Christendom, the lovely Jana Joanna," he said in her ear, quoting her father.

Jana clung to him tightly. "Don't say that," she begged. "I'll cry again. I'm not ready for that—not yet."

"There, there, pet," he said, stroking her hair. "The way he talked about you, I think maybe I was a little bit in love with you back then, before I even met you. But maybe we'd better quit this. You've had enough tumult in the past twenty-four hours." He kissed her ear and the back of her neck. "Let's go sack the Babcock kids' closets to see if we can find something to wear so we can get you out of this ridiculous robe. Then we'll take a look outside and see what the damage is. It sounds as if the storm's dying."

He rose and took her hands, lifting her to her feet. His arms went around her once again and he kissed her lightly on the mouth. "I'd better stop this," he said, his hand under her chin. "I'll want you out of the robe but not back into anything else." But he kissed her one more time, a long time, and her blood hummed with happiness.

AT FIRST, going through other people's closets made Jana feel larcenous, but after rummaging through the garments, discarding one for another, she began to lose her scruples. At last she decided on a pair of thick corduroy jeans and a pair of sweaters, both threadbare at the elbows, but still wearable. "They took all their good clothes," she mourned.

In Mrs. Babcock's closet Jana found an old fur coat. The arms dangled past the ends of her hands like great hairy flippers, but at least it wasn't as voluminous as Zack's robe. She found snow boots as well, too large, but she could stuff the toes.

He left her alone to change in the Babcocks' bedroom, and she shivered as she did so. Her knee was still stiff, but not nearly as painful as it had been the night before. Her muscles still ached slightly, but she felt absurdly content and filled with a sense of well-being.

Zack was waiting for her in the living room, wearing boots and a ski jacket. Sasha danced at his side, frantic with happiness at the prospect of going outside.

"Here," Zack said, holding out her cap and gloves. "I think they're dry. And the wind's stopped. Let's go see just how bad a dude Old Man Winter has been."

He swooped her up in his arms, and Jana laughed in protest.

"What's this? I can still walk!"

"Be quiet and enjoy," he ordered. "The snow's deep. There aren't any paths yet. I'm not going to let you try to wade through it and strain that knee any more. I have my own selfish reasons for nurturing your physical perfection."

He carried her outside, and even under the dull gray sky, Jana blinked at the flawless brightness of the snow. It cloaked all. The solid familiar world of earth and streets was gone, transformed into a chill fantasy, a kingdom of white.

Where bushes had stood, now only white mounds swelled gently; parked cars were merely great heaps of snow. The hedge between their two houses was a swirled drift like a frozen wave. Her back porch had disappeared beneath another drift of white. Tree trunks wore shawls of white on their leeward sides, and the very air sparkled with coldness.

"So this is why you left California," Zack said, his breath warm against her face.

"This is why," she said. "It's terrible, yet there's nothing more beautiful. Except maybe the ice storms. Then all the trees turn to crystal and the whole world sparkles. Everything turns to diamonds. I like weather. California never has weather. It just has day and night. Out here we have weather to spare."

"The hard realities, eh?" He gave her a sardonic smile. "You fled Hollywood for a place where men are men and women are women and weather is weather."

"And movies are only movies," she said, laughing. "That's what I wanted—the middle of America, the middle of what most people think of as life. No glitter, no glitz, no palm trees, just people doing what people have always done. When I first came here, you know what I used to do?"

"Wear a false nose and beard so nobody would know who you were?"

She hit him on the shoulder. "No! I used to drive around and look at the cows grazing in the fields. Sometimes I'd even stop and say, 'Hi, cow. I'm from Hollywood.' They were never impressed. I loved it."

"That's funny," he said, stepping down into the drifts around his porch, holding her carefully. "Whenever I tell a cow who I am, she's usually tremendously impressed. I can't tell you the number of cows who've asked for my autograph. I guess it's my charisma."

Zack waded across the yard carefully, and Jana marveled at the ease with which he carried her. Sasha roistered around them, reveling in the snow. Her bushy tail churned wildly; she frolicked and leaped. She barked with excitement, the sound cracking the crystalline air.

"It's in her blood, the snow," Zack said fondly. "Look at her! Did you ever see such pure joy? It's times like this she's worth all the trouble. This—and last night."

Jana clasped her arms around Zack's neck. "She's a marvelous beast. So are you."

"Thank you, I think." He gave her a look of mock threat. "But watch your tongue, woman. Or I'll drop you in a snowdrift."

"I'll be good," she said with a laugh. "I like it here." She kissed him on the cheek.

"Good grief," he said. "Do you realize what you just did?"

"I think so." She watched her breath plume away into the cold.

"You just kissed me right out here in the open, in front of God and everybody. In a town this size, that probably means we're engaged."

Jana started to smile, but suddenly sobered. The kiss had been spontaneous, natural, but she suddenly wondered if she had lost her mind. She wasn't sure what she was to Zack Devlin at all. She felt so happy with him, so nearly complete that she'd avoided thinking of any tomorrows. The world inside the snowbound house was a world without tomorrows, and all that had mattered was now. Perhaps that's how her father had felt with Tish Farrell those many years ago, forgetting that tomorrows always came.

He hadn't noticed her sudden mental retreat. He was staring down at the seamless white snow that hid the street. "Look," he said, suddenly sober himself. He nodded at the featureless sweep of cold. "That's where you collapsed. You could have been under that. We were damned lucky, sweetheart. Hey! You're shaking again. Come on. Let's go back inside. We can open a can and have Thanksgiving dinner."

He strode back toward the house and Jana was glad. Inside the house was the secure and enchanted world of their own, of the two of them. Sasha followed reluctantly, taking a wild last leap through the drifts.

Inside seemed suddenly warm after the polar air of the snowscape. They ransacked Zack's meager bachelor cupboard and settled on two cans of chili, a box of crackers, and half a stale pound cake for dinner. Sasha was the only one who'd have a proper Thanksgiving feast. Zack had bought her two cans of gourmet dog food.

They sat before the fire, the chili warming in a pot on the coals, and ate crackers. Jana felt warm and safe again, but subdued. Already the November light was fading. She was going to spend another night with Zack Devlin, and she knew that tonight he would not turn away from her as he had done last night. She knew that she did not want him to turn away. What she wanted filled her with a bewildered warmth.

"You've gone quiet on me again," he said, stirring the chili. "Is it because I talked about your father?"

"No," she said. He put his arm around her, and she nestled against the roughness of his sweatered chest. "It was time. I can talk about him again, I think."

He kissed her forehead. "Do you want to talk about him? It might do you good."

She nodded, secure in his nearness. "Yes. I want to," she said, and as the afternoon light faded, she told him about it all. The nights she had made her pillow hot and wet with tears; the reporters lurking at the edge of the schoolyard, shouting questions at her that made her cry; how she could not even go to the drugstore and buy candy without seeing a newspaper or magazine that blared something about her father and Tish Farrell. She told him about how her mother began to drift away from her and Kevvie; the strange attacks of shame and pride that racked her mother—that she wouldn't accept a dime from Kevin O'Dwyer or let him see the children, although she often pointlessly introduced herself to strangers as "Kevin O'Dwyer's first wife, the one he left."

Zack listened, and the calm affection with which he listened kept her from breaking down. Soon their only light was firelight, and when she finished her story at last and looked up at him, seeing his darkly handsome face gilded by the flickering light, she knew she loved him with a power that hurt her because it went so deep. He had freed her from the past. He had given her back her life. The next time he took her in his arms, she knew she could deny him nothing.

The wind began to rise again, but just as it did, the lights flickered, failed, then came to life again. There was a clank and a loud thrumming noise as the furnace came back on.

"Light! Heat!" Jana cried. "I don't believe it!"

"Don't think you're going home," he growled at her, rubbing his sandpaper cheek against hers. "We can lose it again, too. If this storm's a shadow of the last one, those lines won't stay up."

"Who wants to go home?" she said suggestively, and ran her fingers through his black rumpled hair.

His eyes grew suddenly serious. "This is your home, Jana—I mean Charleston, Eastern, the life you made. Would you ever leave it? No. Pretend I never asked that. I'm a bum with a typewriter. I could work anywhere, I guess. I never much thought about settling down anywhere, but a real place with real people and real cows and real weather—a man could think about it."

She felt her heart give a painful tug of happiness. A rush of hope swelled within her. Maybe tomorrows were possible.

Sasha scratched at the door and whined.

Zack groaned. "I'll take her out for a last run. After all, we owe her. Then I'll play you a game of scrabble—there's a set in the kids' bedroom—and I'll beat you at it unmercifully. Then it should be bedtime.''

His golden eyes met hers and held them.

"I guess it will be," she said, her breath tight in her chest.

"Are you sure, Jana?" His voice was husky, his body taut.

"I'm sure," she said, her eyes shining.

He touched her face, then gave a wry smile. His white teeth flashed beneath the black mustache. "In that case, gorgeous," he said, "I'm going out to walk the damned dog."

# CHAPTER TEN

Jana listened to Sasha's barking out in the snow. Night was falling fast, and the dog's cries sounded oddly clear as they broke the strange silence that always seemed to close down on the world when a new snow fell. Then another fresh gust would rise, slamming into the house and rattling the windowpanes.

Zack was opening the door when the phone rang. Jana gave a start; the outside world was reviving all too quickly for her tastes.

"Can you get it?" Zack called, unfastening his snowy boots. Sasha bounded into the house, shaking snow everywhere.

Jana lifted the receiver. "Hello?"

"Hello? Hello? Who is this?" The voice was Nell's and it was quavering with tension. "Jana, is that you? I'm so confused! I rang your place, but nobody answered. Oh, Jana, I've been trying to get somebody, anybody. It's Roger. He came over to check on me, the old fool, as if I couldn't take care of myself. Oh, Jana. He walked through all that snow, at his age! And now he's here and he's ill. He's having chest pains. I'm afraid he's having a heart attack, and I can't get through to anyone. Half the lines are still out, and the hospital lines are jammed. I don't know what to do."

"Steady, Nell, keep calm," Jana said, but she felt a wave of dismay. It must have shown on her face, because Zack was at her side, a frown knitting his dark brows.

"What's wrong?"

"It's Nell. She thinks Roger's having a heart attack," Jana said, her voice shaking.

"Here." Zack took the phone from her hand. "Nell, this is Zack. Where are you? Where's Roger? What are his symptoms? Good, keep him lying down. Don't let him get up. I don't know, hit him on the head if you have to. Have you got any whiskey over there? Give him a sip. I'm on my way over. Don't panic. But keep trying to get through to the hospital. Don't worry, Nell, I'm on my way."

Another gust of wind shook the house.

"I'm going over," he said, his face grim. He turned up the collar of his jacket.

"Oh, Zack, you can't!" Jana protested. "Listen to it out there. It could be worse than last night."

"I've got to," he said. "She can't handle this alone. And somebody's got to get him to the hospital."

"But how? You'll never get your car out. The streets aren't even cleared. You could be—"

"If he has to get to a hospital, I'll get him to a hospital if I have to carry him on my back. You stay here. If the heat goes off again, there are plenty of logs. I'll try to get back to you as soon as I can."

"I'm going with you!" she said, turning to get her coat, but his hand shot out and closed on her arm.

"No." His voice was implacable. "Not on that game knee. Don't argue. You'd only slow me down. I can't worry about you and Roger both. You're staying put. Sash will keep you company. I'll call you from Nell's. Stay warm, darling."

He bent over her and gathered her into his arms. His lips took hers with a hungry desperation, his tongue flickering like a flame against her own. With sensuous mastery his lips pressed hers, his hand sliding over her body. Languor and warmth flooded her. She did not want him to go away, not now, not ever.

His kiss dominated and demanded, and she yielded to it freely. But then he drew away. "I'll never get there at this rate," he sighed, his voice rough. "I could do this all night, and I intend to, as soon as possible. Take care."

"Zack—be careful," she pleaded. Her face tingled from the scrape of his unshaven beard, and her lips felt ripely swollen. "You will be careful?"

"If you think a measly blizzard is going to keep you safe from me, think again," he said, shooting her a dark grin. "I think you've generated enough heat in my body so that I can melt the snow all the way to Nell's. They ought to bottle 'Essence of Jana' and send it to all those poor explorers stuck on the South Pole. They could frisk over the ice cap in their underwear."

He tugged on his boots, wound a muffler around his neck and pulled his gloves from his pocket.

"You don't even have a hat," she wailed.

"Hats are for girls and sissies," he said, grinning. "Don't worry. Come here."

She stepped toward him and he put his arms around her. "Are you my girl?"

She nodded up to him happily, her friends the butterflies looping the loop inside her.

"Then what could happen to me? The worst is that I freeze off my mustache, and I won't let that happen. I think it stimulates you. I'm going to give you a very short kiss goodbye, and when I come back I'll give you some very long ones. Maybe they'll be all night long."

Again his lips possessed hers, dazing her with the intensity of the feelings he awakened. The sureness of his mouth upon her own made her feel as if flowers were blooming in her brain, profuse as the desires that swept her.

"Don't worry," he said, smiling again, and then he was gone. Sasha whined and scratched against the door, her yellow eyes disturbed.

"Come on, girl," Jana said, leading her by the collar back to the couch. "I don't like it any better than you do. Come up here by me and we'll worry together."

She curled up on the couch, and the dog leaped up easily and sat beside her, but gave a soft whimper. Jana put her arms around the furry neck and pressed her face against Sash's bristly coat. "He can take care of himself," she said. "Nothing could ever hurt him." The dog whined again, unconvinced.

Each slap of the wind against the house now sounded immense and sinister. Outside the windows the sky was black, and when at last Jana went to the front door and turned on the porch light, the illumination shone on swirling snow, riding thick on the twisting wind.

She paced, and the dog paced with her. She went to the kitchen to make coffee, and Sasha padded behind her. She sat on the couch and drank the coffee, and the dog lay with its head in her lap. Each tick of the clock on the Babcocks' mantel sounded strident. Each blast of wind rocked the house and made it creak.

She kept looking at the clock and forgetting what time it had been when she looked at it last. Nell's house was almost a mile away. How long would he take to reach there? Had he already been gone an hour? Or was it longer?

When the phone finally rang, she leaped so swiftly to get it that Sasha barked at her. "Hello?" she said, her heart hammering.

The voice was Zack's, clipped and grim. "I'm at Nell's. I would have got here sooner, but I had to stop and steal a car. Roger's had some kind of cardiac incident, and I'm going to try to get him to the hospital."

"You stole a car? I don't understand."

"It's brutal out there," he said. "I realized if Roger needed help, I was going to need transportation. I found just what I needed—a Land Rover fitted with a snow blade parked in somebody's driveway. They probably run a little snowplowing business on the side. Nobody home, so I drew upon my misspent youth, broke into it and hot-wired it. The owner's probably finishing up Thanksgiving dinner somewhere in St. Louis with his dear old mother, unaware a former street punk from Chino has made off with his wheels."

Jana smiled in spite of her worry. "Resourceful, aren't you?"

"Let's just say that maybe sometimes crime does pay," he replied. "But I've got to get cracking. Nell's bundling up Roger. I've got to get him to the hospital. The phone lines are still a mess. It took me three tries to get through to you. Are the lights and heat still on?"

"So far so good," she said. Sasha, pressed against her leg, whined.

"I don't know how long this is going to take," he said. "The streets are terrible. A few plows have gone through, but the snow drifts back as fast as they doze it out. I'll call you from the hospital. If I don't get back, sleep in my bed. It's got an electric blanket. And Jana—''

"Yes?"

"I love you."

"I love you, too," she breathed. The words sounded strange and wonderful to her.

"Bye, baby," he said, and she heard the click of his hanging up.

She blushed, wondering if Nell had heard him say that he loved her. She hoped not; there would be some hard explaining to do.

The wind roared outside. Sasha returned to the couch and curled up on it neatly, her tail covering her snout. She looked at Jana as if to say, "When's he coming home? What's he doing now? Will he be all right?"

"I don't know," Jana said. She listened to the wind and wondered herself. How far was it from Nell's to Lincoln Hospital? Three miles? Four? Would the highway even be open?

It was another hour before the phone rang again. Jana pounced on it.

"Roger's going to be fine," Zack announced. "I want you to call Nell and tell her, all right? I can't tie up a phone here. It's a madhouse. It wasn't a full-fledged heart attack—angina pains, the doctor said. He should be home in a couple of days, good as new if he watches himself."

"Thank God," Jana breathed.

"But they need me here, babe. One of the ambulances slid and crashed into another one. They need help answering the calls. I volunteered. This place is a zoo. Doctors exhausted and nurses dead on their feet. And all over town there are people like Roger who overdid it and babies deciding it's time to be born, blizzard or none, and a hundred other things. I don't know when I'll be back."

"Zack, be careful. Don't try to be a hero. Just get back when you can, okay?"

"I'm no hero," he taunted. "Besides, there's a hell of a story in this—town rallies against blizzard of the century and all that good stuff. I smell news."

For some reason, the familiar ring of cynicism in his voice comforted her.

"I've got to get off the phone," he said, and she could hear the confusion of noises in the background.

"Be careful," she repeated.

"You forget whom you're dealing with," he said. "Bye, love."

Jana dialed Nell and told her Roger was in no danger. Nell was obviously trying hard to keep from crying.

"I was never so glad to see a man in my life when Zack came through that door," she said. "He looked like he'd fought his way clear from the North Pole. And a Jeep, or something—he even managed to get a Jeep. Roger scared me to death. He said his phone was out and he was worried about me. Can you imagine that? Roger actually worried about somebody? But he should have known better, exerting himself like that. But what are you doing at Zack's place? Are you all right?"

"He has a fireplace. I don't." Jana said, choosing to substitute part of the truth for the whole. "How about you?"

"Well, I was chilly, of course, but I have a fireplace and a gas range. I stoked up the fire and kept on the oven and was getting along just fine. My biggest worry was what was I going to do with all that food I bought for Thanksgiving. Do you know how many radishes I've got? Maybe I can still have the students over another time, but what do I do with all these radishes and things in the meantime? And this turkey? What does a single woman do with a twenty-five-pound turkey? Thank heaven it never quite thawed out. No, it's mostly the radishes, all cut into rosettes. I'm up to my neck in radish roses.''

Jana let Nell dither on, working out her nervousness. She knew full well that Nell was worried about Roger, not radishes, but the human mind did peculiar things under stress.

At last Nell ran out of steam, confessing she was exhausted and going to bed. ''And be sure to thank Zack again for me, dear. It was more than good of him, it was terribly brave. I suppose it must be very strange for you staying in a man's house like that, but I'm sure he's a perfect gentleman, and Les will understand.''

Jana smiled at the idea of Zack Devlin being a perfect gentleman. But the mention of Les's name struck her abruptly. She had forgotten he even existed. What would he say? Or would he even care?

She said goodbye to Nell and went and stood by the window. The wind seemed to be dying, its assaults less frequent and less forceful. She was, like Nell, emotionally exhausted. She thought of Zack out somewhere in the snow and the blackness, fighting the Land Rover away from the hospital and back again. She didn't want to go to sleep until he was home again, and she could touch him, making sure he was safe and real. It was strange. He really hadn't been gone so long, but she was lonely for him.

Sometime after midnight, she realized she could stay awake no longer. She went to his bedroom, and the dog sauntered along behind her, a guilty look in her eyes.

"I bet you're not supposed to sleep on the bed," Jana said, eyeing Sasha's laid back ears. "You don't fool me a bit. You're a terrible liar. But what the heck. It's just us girls. We'll have a slumber party."

She switched on the electric blanket. The room was really the Babcocks', and it showed little of Zack Devlin's personality. A typing table with a new electric typewriter on it stood near the window, and Jana felt a wave of guilt, remembering how she'd ruined his other typewriter that day, and the way she'd met him.

She undressed, switched off the light and climbed between the sheets. Crisp, they smelled faintly of Zack's cologne, and she stretched luxuriously. Sasha curled on the foot of the bed with a sigh of contentment. Jana felt strange, alone in his bed. She fell asleep hugging his pillow.

An odd sound awoke her the next morning. Silence. Her eyes fluttered open. The wind had died. She jumped out of bed, pulled on her clothing and ran to the window. It was too thickly covered with frost to reveal anything, so she scratched a peephole. Impossibly, the sun was shining. It glittered with eye-piercing brightness on the fresh waves and drifts of snow.

She glanced at the digital clock on the dresser. It was almost seven o'clock, and Zack still wasn't back. She went downstairs to make sure he hadn't come home and fallen asleep on the couch out of sheer exhaustion.

But the downstairs rooms were empty and echoing. Sasha whined at the door to get out. Jana donned her borrowed fur coat, her borrowed boots, her cap and gloves and took Sasha out. Her knee hardly pained her at all, and suddenly, playing with the dog in the sunshine and sparkling snow, life seemed very good indeed. If only Zack were there it would have been perfect.

She played with Sasha until her knee began to throb, then cajoled the dog back into the house. She'd have a hot shower, then see what she could find in the way of breakfast for herself and for Zack when he got home. She found a coffee maker in the kitchen and started a pot of strong brew. She went into the boys' bedrooms, prowling for clean clothes, and then went for her shower.

The stinging water felt wonderful, and she turned it on as hot as she could stand it. One of her "lobster showers," Kevvie had used to call them, when she steamed up the bathroom like fog rolling in off the ocean and emerged from the water with a pink tingling glow.

She went into the kitchen, switched on the radio and had a cup of coffee while the newscaster droned on about the storm: "Twenty-three inches of snow in some areas, up to thirty in others; travelers marooned, cars abandoned, electricity off over most of Charleston for twenty-eight hours, but we're digging out, folks. The old Midwestern gumption saw us through. We'll be back on our feet in no time flat."

Jana glanced at the kitchen clock. Zack had been gone for almost fifteen hours. Surely he was all right, and surely he'd be home soon. She had already heard the rumble of the city snowplows cutting through the eerie silence, plowing Lincoln Highway. She tried not to fidget, to keep busy. She washed the dishes she and Zack had used, mopped counters and straightened the living room. She remembered she hadn't made the bed and went back to his room.

She tucked in the sheets, smoothed out the blanket, returned the plaid bedspread over the blanket and plumped pillows.

She wandered to the window and rubbed a larger peephole in the front. Sasha followed her, as usual.

"Now I know what they mean when they say somebody dogs your steps," Jana said to her. Sasha wagged. Outside, the snow still flashed its blinding glitter, but the street was deserted.

Her eyes fell to the typewriter on the table. A paper was in the carriage; her eyes took in the words automatically.

And then the realization of what she'd read struck her like a blow.

On the right-hand top of the page was typed *"Fame's Children page 329."* The page began in midsentence:

...overindulged by a doting father. She had neither the character nor the courage to survive his desertion of her. She fled from the memory of that desertion, but in ways that were uniquely her own. Some might say her escape was less desperate than her brother's, but they underestimate the extent to which she retreated from reality. She hoped to evade the memory of the Hollywood years by taking refuge in a small town, an ordinary life, but she could never trust men again. Hopelessly naive...

The page ended there. He must have been typing it when the storm hit.

The bastard, she thought. The lying bastard. He'd been lying all the time. He was writing about her and Kevvie and she'd almost—she'd wanted to—Oh, God, Jana thought. Hopelessly naive, was she? Retreating from reality, was she? Couldn't relate to men, could she?

She punched the typewriter's On key, felt it purr into life, rolled the paper up a few inches and with shaking fingers typed, "If you ever come near me again, I'll scratch your eyes out. If hate could kill, you'd be dead before you could read this." She didn't bother to sign her name.

She charged from the bedroom. Sasha began barking wildly. "Shut up, you!" Jana said, fighting back tears of anger. She ran to the bathroom, snatching up her running suit, which Zack had hung on a rack to dry. She'd worry about getting the Babcocks' clothes back to them later, when the Babcocks themselves were back.

She grabbed her running shoes from in front of the fire and heard the door open. Sasha was bounding around in excitement, making noises of greeting.

Then Zack was there, blocking her way. He stepped toward her and put his arms around her, laying his cheek against her hair. She was too rigid with anger to trust herself to make any response. She only could marvel at his audacity.

"What a night," he said, his voice weary. "I had to push that damned thing out of drifts three times. Oh, babe, is it good to be home."

"I'm sure it is," she said bitterly. "I'll be going now. Thanks for all your...hospitality." She spat the word out as if it were poison and pushed away from him.

"Jana! What's wrong?" His face was ravaged with tiredness and he stared at her without comprehension.

"Get out of my life," she said evenly, "and stay out." She tried to make her way past him, but his hands flew out and pulled her to him with a roughness that surprised her.

"What the hell is this?" he asked, glaring down at her. The stubble on his face was heavier this morning, and it made him look like a pirate. "What's wrong with you?"

"I don't owe you any explanations, you snake," she said contemptuously. "I said I wanted you out of my life and I meant it, you low-life...you...you—"

"I don't know what kind of bee you've got in your bonnet, Jana," he said, suddenly letting go of her. "And to tell the truth, I'm a little too tired to stand around begging for an explanation. So either tell me or—"

"Go to blazes!" she hurled at him. "And don't play the weary hero with me! You're a lousy hack and you always will be! I hope you saw a lot of good stuff last night, so you can fly back to your vulture's nest and turn it into easy money."

"Oh, look," he said, his voice suddenly dangerous. "If you're mad because I stayed out there last night—"

"You could have stayed out there forever, and it'd be no loss to me!" But the flash of anger in his eyes made her back away a step.

"Jana, I wanted to be with you last night. But I could hardly—"

"Who needs you?" she said, suddenly giving in to her fury. "I don't! Who wants you? I don't. I hate you!"

She felt tears stinging her eyes, but she would rather die in front of him than let him see her cry. She stalked past him, and this time he didn't try to stop her.

She grabbed up the tattered fur coat and flung it around herself. She snatched her cap and gloves.

"Are you crazy?" he yelled after her. "What is this?"

But she cut off his voice with the slam of the front door and began to thrash her way across the snow to her own house.

She yanked open her door and stamped inside. She felt sick with anger and shame. Almost immediately the phone began to ring. She picked it up.

Zack's voice said, "Would you mind telling me—" She sent the receiver crashing down, then took the phone off the hook.

She would not cry. She refused to. She had to keep her head clear. She had to think about so many things. About getting a lawyer, for instance. A high-powered one.

She went into the bathroom to splash cold water on her face and groaned when the pipes shuddered and nothing came out. She kicked the base of the sink. What else could go wrong? A pipe must have frozen and burst. She'd go to Nell's. She'd walk. The snowplows were out and if she stayed with the main streets, she could make it easily.

She dialed Nell's number and told her about the pipes. Nell, sensing that Jana was upset, insisted she come right over.

Then Zack Devlin was banging on her back door. "Sounds like you've got company, dear," Nell said. "See you soon. Are you sure you can make it over all right?"

"I'm sure," Jana said grimly. She hung up and turned to the back door. "Go away or I'll call the police," she shouted. "I mean it! If I had a gun, I'd shoot you, you vermin."

"Jana!" he shouted back. "Would you please tell me—"

"I said go away! Or I'll boil oil and pour it on you!"

"Do you want me to kick this damned door down?"

"I'm calling the police," she threatened. "My hand is on the phone. I mean it."

"Jana, I am too damned tired for this foolishness. What in hell is wrong with you?"

"You're wrong with me," she cried. "Now get out of here, or I *will* call the police. I mean it."

His voice was suddenly disgusted and filled with fatigue.

"Jana, if I get in there, you may *need* the police. Because I'll wring your pretty neck. I haven't had any sleep for thirty hours, and I spent about eighteen of those hours fighting the snow. I'm going home and I'm going to bed, and when I wake up, I'm coming over here, and I'll drag you out by the hair if I have to. Unless you've come to your senses by then."

He gave the doorframe a mighty whack that made the glass shiver. "I mean it," he threatened.

He wheeled and stalked off.

She turned away and went into her bedroom to begin throwing things into her overnight case.

She waited until she thought he surely must have fallen asleep, so he couldn't come out of the house and try to force-feed her more of his lies.

She grabbed the overnight case and her purse and locked the door behind her. Her knee ached, but she ignored it. The walk through the snow to Nell's seemed to take no time at all, her mind was so consumed by Zack Devlin's slimy duplicity. How stupid could she have been? She'd been right at first. Devlin was no good and passion was no good and love was only a way of making people terminally silly.

"Jana!" Nell said, opening the door. "How pink your cheeks are! Uh, wherever did you get the...fur coat?"

Jana looked down, embarrassed. She'd been so outraged, she'd forgotten to take off Mrs. Babcock's aged fur or the old boots.

"Come in, come in," Nell fussed. "Did Zack get back? Did you thank him again for me? I must do something for him. I—"

"Don't ever mention that man's name to me again," Jana said, her eyes blazing. "I mean it, Nell. I know he helped Roger out, but please, never, never mention his name to me again!"

Nell looked at her with alarm. "Why, Jana! But he— Oh, dear, he must have done something improper. Did he? I mean, I thought surely he must be a gentleman, but the human heart is such a curious mixture of good and bad, I'm sure I don't...I hardly know what—"

"Please," Jana begged. "Just don't say anything about him. And if he calls up here asking about me, tell him you don't know anything. Promise?"

"You mean lie to him? After all he did for—"

"Please!" Jana insisted. "Promise me."

"Well, all right, if you insist. Oh, this is terrible. I wish Les were here. He'd thrash that man within an inch of his life. Not that I could stand by and watch. I mean I do owe..oh, my. This is something. Sit down, dear. You're all upset."

"Nell," Jana said suddenly. "I'm going to get married. I'm going to tell Les I'll marry him when he comes back. I think it's the most sensible thing I could do. I know it is."

"Well, I'm sure it is if you say so," Nell fluttered, "but are you quite yourself today?"

"Yes," Jana said firmly. "I'm myself. Again. Thank heaven. I didn't mean to force myself and my problems on you, but if he calls, you won't tell him I'm here, will you?"

"If that's what you want," Nell said. "And I've had such a time of it myself, I'm glad of the company. Besides," she said brightly, with the nervous logic peculiar to Nell alone, "you can help me eat all those radishes. Do you like radishes, dear?"

Jana nodded numbly, but she wasn't thinking of radishes. She was thinking of golden eyes and a black mustache, the scrape of a stubbled cheek against her own.

Yes, marrying Les would be the most sensible thing she could do. And it would serve her right.

# CHAPTER ELEVEN

AFTER THE FIRST HOT WAVES of anger subsided, Jana was filled with a sick emptiness. She presumed on Nell's hospitality for four days, as another storm postponed classes. She couldn't go back to her own house until she captured the creature that had become Charleston's most elusive—a plumber. An epidemic of frozen pipes made plumbers as hard to find as whooping cranes, and it was just as well because Jana didn't want to go back home anyway.

Nell was sweet, but in a state of confusion, always saying things such as "Well, dear, I know that you don't want to talk about it, but if you do want to talk about it, I'd be glad to talk about it. Because Zack Devlin certainly has his good side, even if he has his bad side, and maybe whatever he did wasn't so terrible. After all, he is a normal healthy man with normal urges. But who am I to say? I'm sure you know your own mind, dear. But are you quite certain? No, don't answer. I'm not going to pry."

Jana felt she was being driven slightly crazy, and she developed a loathing for radishes she was sure would last a lifetime.

Roger was just as bad. Jana didn't go to see him, but she talked to him twice a day on the phone. She was afraid Zack would show up at the hospital, and she was right. Nell came home from visits positively fizzing with the desire to tell Jana about Zack and what he'd said and what he'd asked about Jana.

"What's wrong with you?" Roger rasped across the phone line. "Talk to the man. What'd you do to him? He looks like a storm cloud on legs. First time I saw him, I thought, now there's a man for Jana. Not that piece of ice milk currently melting in Egypt, who's only in love with your paycheck."

"Roger," Jana said as gently as she could, for Roger was sick, even if he didn't sound like it, "Les is really very suitable for me. I have no interest in Zack Devlin. I wish you wouldn't talk about him."

"I nearly died! I've been at death's door," Roger stormed. "I'll say what I please. If you're going to marry somebody, at least make it a man and not a carp. Somebody with blood in his veins, not that cold fish, that halibut. Now be quiet. I know you're going to tell me it's none of my business and I'm being offensive. Let me tell you when I was next door to dying I was overcome with regret for all the offensive things I'd left unsaid in my lifetime. Besides, I'm still sick, so I get to be as offensive as I want to be."

The only way she could get him to stop was to ask him about the nurses and the hospital food, two topics on which Roger tended to have some extremely offensive things to say.

Zack called for Jana at Nell's repeatedly at first, but after Nell's first attempts at dissimulation, she gave up. She could only sputter that she was sorry as could be, but Jana had made up her mind apparently, and there was nothing Nell could do about it.

Twice he appeared at Nell's door, but Jana, by some inner warning system she didn't understand, knew it was Zack almost before he knocked and fled into Nell's guest bedroom. Jana knew the only reason he didn't come in and rip the bedroom door off its hinges was that it was Nell's house.

After two days, he stopped trying. Maybe he'd found her note by then and given up his pretense of outraged innocence. He knew she'd found him out and his game was up. She was relieved when he stopped calling, stopped coming to Nell's house. Knowing he had been there, so near, with all the old silken lies, had hurt her almost more than she could stand.

If what she felt was merely hate, she could have borne it, but she was stunned to realize that her emotions were deeper, more complex and far more traitorous. Zack Devlin had betrayed her, but he had also awakened desire in her, and it was as if he had poisoned her and she would never be well again.

She wondered if this was how her father had felt about Tish Farrell—a relentless longing for what you knew was wrong for you, for what could destroy you as surely as a bullet, but not with a bullet's merciful speed. It destroyed you from the inside out, so that you died standing up, like a tree, eaten from within by a yearning that killed you day by day, hour by hour, minute by minute.

She wanted him back, she realized with utter hopelessness. Not the way he was, but the way he had seemed for that time in the house, when the storm insulated them from the outside world, from reality itself. She wanted the Zack Devlin who could be gentle but at the same time dizzy her with his ardor, the man who sat by the fire, his arms around her, a joke or a word of love on his chiseled lips.

She wanted that, she knew, and the knowledge gnawed at her. Worse, even knowing what he was—a liar, a con artist, a cheat—didn't change the physical response he stirred in her, the desire that coursed like a dangerous electrical charge throughout her body. He had done all this to her, and she had let it be done, and all he ever wanted was her one shabby little secret so he could set it before a world that would leave dirty fingerprints all over her life.

She was seven kinds of a fool, and that oppressed her more than Zack's betrayal. Somehow she had managed to fall in love with a man who had never existed, the Zack who had existed only for the duration of the storm. She could still feel waves of longing for the man who had used her with only cold calculation.

In spite of what she'd said to Nell and Roger, she knew she could never marry Les, not feeling as she did now. She would never marry anybody. She'd throw herself into her work and try to recover from the addictive, toxic sweetness of love. She had done it before, in a different way, with her father, and she could do it again.

By Tuesday morning the plumbers had performed whatever mysteries plumbers perform, and she moved back into her house.

Classes resumed, and she did double time by taking over two of Roger's courses until the doctors said he was well enough to go back to work. She studiously avoided running into Zack. He returned the compliment.

On Friday she caught a glimpse of him walking down the hall. Her heart contracted as if squeezed by a fist of ice. His dark head was bent over a sleek blond one, and with a jolt, Jana recognized Christine.

*Well, what did you expect?* she asked herself. *You knew about her before. This weekend it's Christine in Zack's bed, and their pillow talk would be about how much money his book of dirty little secrets would make them both.* Jana thought for the thousandth time about finding a lawyer, but suddenly felt too tired to think of fighting.

She went into her office and closed the door. For once in her life she was grateful for the stacks of papers to be graded.

She worked for an hour, trying to get her mind focused on news hooks and comma splices, when a knock at the door destroyed the concentration she had been struggling to center.

"Come in," she said, sure it was yet another of Roger's nervous students, wondering if Roger was coming back, when Roger was coming back, and what was she planning to do about grades in the meantime.

The door opened, and Jana was half-dismayed, half-angry at seeing Christine. So Zack had sent a woman to do his fighting for him.

Christine had come to threaten and cajole about the book, to tell her not to try to fight. Maybe she and Zack were even cold-blooded enough to try to offer her a piece of the action—fight us and you'll lose everything. After all, as soon as you step into court, Jana, the secret's out, and everybody knows who you are. Be quiet, be a good girl, and we'll cover up your real name and give you a cut of the profits.

"We need to talk," Christine said, her eyes appraising. "I have the feeling you may not like the idea, and I'm not crazy about finding myself in this position, either. Nonetheless, we need to straighten some matters out. May I sit down?"

Jana nodded curtly toward the chair that students used when they came in for conferences. Christine lowered herself into it with all the obvious disdain of a queen forcing herself to sit on a park bench. She shot a glance of distaste around the cramped office.

"They don't give you much space, do they?" Christine asked, eyeing the filing cabinets that hulked against the walls.

"I work with my mind," Jana said. "I've got all the working space I need right here...." She gestured with her pencil at her curls. "If you need a shuffleboard court or something, I suggest you go to the park."

"Hmm. Zack was right. You have an absolutely filthy sharp tongue. Mind if I smoke? Not that I mind if you mind, but I do observe forms enough to ask."

"Smoke up a veritable storm," Jana said, pushing her ashtray across the desk. "I've smelled worse things than smoke. Especially lately."

"Zack's right again. You're not only sharp-tongued, you're impossible," Christine purred. "But let's not fence, darling. I've made a long and tedious trip from New York, mostly because of you."

"You didn't have to bother," Jana said. She wondered which would come first—threats or bribes.

"I did have to bother," Christine said, lighting a cigarette. "Zack has a book he desperately needs to finish. You're keeping him from finishing it. I don't like it when my writers don't produce."

Jana studied her in silence. Christine evinced her usual icy perfection. Her pale hair glimmered under the office lights. Her expensive suit of gray wool matched the frosty grayness of her eyes. She must play snow leopard to Zack's pantherlike grace.

"Say what you have to say. And make it fast. I'm busy."

"You're busy being a fool," Christine said, blowing out a stream of blue smoke. "You don't understand a single thing that's happened. Neither does Zack. But of course this is a new experience for him. My business is books and big bucks, not romantic counseling. But to honor your request and make it fast, Zack's mad for you, and you're mad for him obviously, or you couldn't be so furious at him. You're both stubborn creatures with an absolute genius for getting under each other's skin. You think he's trying to write about you, don't you?"

"I don't think so," Jana said coolly. "I know so. And I don't care if you threaten to line lawyers by the battalion up against me, I'll block you. I don't care how much I get hurt in the process, either, so don't try to warn me about that. That book will never seen print, I guarantee you."

Christine laughed throatily. "Well, I see what the charm is. He's finally met somebody as pigheaded as himself. A match made in heaven, if the gods have a larky sense of humor. You really are a spitfire, you know. And you've got him in a perfect state. He doesn't even know why...but his imagination is fertile enough to supply a thousand impossible reasons, all unflattering to you, I might add. His latest theory is you're mad because you think he left you sitting in that storm, and you're a selfish, irrational little witch.''

"What do you mean, he doesn't know?" Jana shot back. "Oh, he knows. I left him word. In no uncertain terms—"

"Do you mean this?" Christine asked. She opened a folder and took out the paper that had been in Zack's typewriter, the page on which Jana had written her acid note of farewell.

Jana looked at it, remembering that afternoon and the staggering sensations of loss and betrayal. "Yes," she finally said. "What of it?"

"The 'what of it' is, for your information, that he never got it." Christine rummaged in the folder and drew out a stack of typed sheets. "He hasn't gone near his typewriter since your little blowup. I doubt he ever noticed this, and if he did he was too distraught to make the connection. I slipped into his room this morning while he was shaving, just to check how far he'd got with the revisions, and I found this. I've not only had to play romantic counselor, but detective as well. Neither role suits me. I'm far too selfish. I'd rather be sitting in my office drawing up fat contracts, or at home in my own bed, not camping out in some child's bedroom in Illinois. Why do little boys insist on tacking posters of monsters all over their walls? It's revolting. One can hardly sleep with seven extraterrestrials from *Star Wars* glaring down on one.''

Jana's head ached. She thought she'd anticipated all the approaches Christine could take with her, but this one confused her. Was the woman trying to claim she wasn't Zack's mistress?

"I mention the bed on purpose," Christine said, seeming to read her thoughts. "No, I'm not having an affair with Zack. He's not my type. Quite frankly, I'm not a highly sexed person. I eschew the more volatile passions. I've always thought sex was basically nature's way of providing amusement for those not smart enough to play the stock market."

"I don't understand what you're trying to do," Jana said carefully. She wanted to believe Christine, but she'd been hurt too often to hope again.

"What I'm trying to do is clear up all the misunderstanding so my best but most stubborn writer will finish his revisions. You didn't read the pages before the one in the typewriter. They're about Holly Holliday. A child star in the early days of Hollywood. Which is what the whole book's about—all those odious little moppets of the silent screen. Zack hated the project from the beginning. I practically had to hold a gun on him to make him do it. The publisher wanted some revisions and that, in part, was what he was supposed to be doing here. Take a look."

She thrust the pages at Jana:

Holly and her brother Perry were hot stuff until they reached puberty and got uncute. Their father was a vaudevillian who came to Tinsel Town to make his fortune. He made it through the kids. A casting agent spotted Holly and Perry, and Dear Old Dad's financial problems were over. Except just about the same time Holly's career went into a slide, Dear Old Dad died. He died when Holly was fifteen and still trying to play a six-year-old in hair ribbons and sausage curls. She viewed his death as a desertion. Any psychiatrist can tell you how often that happens. She never got over it. Neither did her brother, who ultimately got involved with what is vulgarly called "the mob."

"The idea for this book was mine," Christine continued. "Zack hated it. He particularly hated dealing with the Holly Holliday story because it's so pathetic. He wanted to cut it, but the pubisher wanted it lengthened. Poor Holly. She was still a child when she was sixty-eight, Jana. The sausage curls, the incredible naiveté, living out her life in the little town in Kansas where her father had been born. Maybe she thought she could appease her father's ghost and bring him back if she remained a cute little girl forever. Or maybe she thought she'd really managed to stop time, and she was living the part that she'd made famous—that darling little American sweetheart. Not a pretty story.

"Even though he loathed the idea, Zack finally agreed to the book because he thought it might sell. It would give him enough money to try another one of those dreary presidential books he so loves. This time about Lincoln."

Jana's eyes widened. "Lincoln?" She still was uncertain about believing Christine, but the pages in her hand were real, and the story they told was Holly Holiday's, not her own.

"Abraham Lincoln. Especially his relationship to his stepmother, his 'angel mother' as he called her. She lived here, of course." Christine sighed, as if with boredom.

"Of course," Jana breathed. Sara Lincoln had lived here. The hospital was even named for her. And one of

Lincoln's famous debates had taken place here. It all fitted together. That is, most of it fitted together. Jana frowned.

"But how did you know?" Jana asked. "How did you know what I thought? Did he tell you who I was? About my father?"

"You really are obsessed, aren't you? No. I told him."

Jana stared at her, bewildered.

"When he was so determined to come here, I told him you were here. I knew about his interest in your father. I certainly didn't think it would hurt for him to look you up. And if you want to know how I knew, let's just say I have connections in the strangest places. Last spring I got a letter from a man in this area, proposing a book about your father, with the angle of how the famous scandal had affected his daughter. He said he was going to Egypt and hadn't decided whether he wanted to write the book or not, but he'd know by the end of the year. He wanted to know how much it would be worth."

"Les!" Jana said. "It was Les! He knew. He's the only one who knew! The only one I ever told."

"From his letter, it didn't seem as if he could write his way out of a paper bag. The whole thing smelled fishy. I told him so. I told him Kevin O'Dwyer wasn't a story anyway."

Jana groaned and put her head in her hands. "That rotten fink. If he couldn't use me for his career one way, he'd do it another...."

"That was his name—Lester something," Christine said, lighting another cigarette. "But I'd recommend you stop sitting there kicking yourself over Les or whoever he happens to be and get to the business at hand. Which is Zack, who is my business. You too, by the way, if you ever want anybody to handle your material. You could probably write quite a decent book. I've seen a few of your pieces. Right now, however, if I were you, I'd go knock on Zack's door. He's home, and I've rented a car this time and am driving myself to the airport, so I can drop you off on the way. I told him his mood is absolutely too vile to bear.''

Jana spread her fingers and peered at Christine. "But how can I explain all this to him? He has every right to be furious. I must have seemed crazy to him. After he'd been out all night, risking his life..."

"Don't bore me with the details of Zack's long snowy night," Christine said. "Zack's deeds of civic service aren't my concern. What he puts on paper is. So give him this. It explains things more succinctly than you'll probably be able to. And give him the manuscript. The man's not dull. He'll catch on. And then, I hope to heaven he'll get back to work."

She handed Jana the last sheet of paper in the folder. "You might as well read it," she said. "That's how you got yourself into this mess—peeping into other people's writing."

Jana blushed, looking down at the paper covered with Christine's elegant scrawl:

Zack, you boob. You write about Holly Holiday in such ambiguous and vague language that it's no wonder the poor girl thought you were writing about her and O'Dwyer. Either shape up your prose or tell me to go to war with the publisher so we can drop the chapter.

Christine.

P.S. I still think a book on Lincoln is a lousy idea.

Jana put all the papers together and stood up. "I don't know how to thank you," she began, shaking her head. "And I was really very rude to you. I guess I can only say—"

"If you want to thank me, get him to finish the damned revisions. And stop being excessively grateful. Excessive gratitude is the most embarrassing of emotions. It distresses me, and I hate to be distressed. I will give you a ride to Zack's only if you will restrain yourself from being excessively grateful. Then I'm driving that loathsome rental car to the airport and escaping from all this clean sparkling snow and fresh air. It oppresses me. I want the slush and pollution that are a New Yorker's birthright."

She rose from the chair, looking down at Jana and shaking her sleek head in wonder. "The things I have to do to turn a profit," she sighed.

Jana's heart was dancing by the time they settled in the car. It was doing several kinds of dances at once, not the least of which was a dance of fear. But it was also managing to execute a manic tap dance of sheer joy.

"Are you really as cold as you pretend?" Jana asked, grinning at Christine's perfect profile.

"Oh, no, my dear," Christine said evenly, as they crossed Lincoln Highway. "I'm actually much colder. And Zack's never been anything more to me than a client, although I do like the dog. I'm a sucker for dogs. I have three myself. So much more dependable than people. Ah, there they are now, frisking in the snow. When Zack's in an intolerable mood, he tends to frisk a great deal, and I've never understood the logic of it at all."

Zack and Sasha were rolling in a snowdrift as the car pulled up in front of the house. He stood, staring at the car with a frown on his face, the dark brows pulled together. Sasha took a leap toward the car, but he grabbed her collar. His jeans and the blue jacket he wore were covered with snow, and snow gleamed in his black hair. Jana thought he had never looked so handsome, with his lean hips and broad shoulders, his breath pluming out from beneath the dark mustache.

"Ta-ta," Christine said, lifting one penciled eyebrow. Jana shot her a smile and unlocked the door. She ran across the snow, waving the pages Christine had given her.

Sasha tried to twist away from Zack to greet her.

"I was wrong," Jana yelled, floundering through the snow toward him. "I made a mistake! I'm sorry!"

"What the hell?" he snarled. "What are you doing with Christine? Go away. You're a crazy lady. I'm sick of chasing you around, and just when I think I've finally got you, you turn on me like a psychopath. What is this?"

She thrust the pages at him. "Christine wrote you a note. And said to give you back your manuscript."

He snatched the pages from her. "And what are you doing with my manuscript? What is this, Jana?" His face was dark with anger, but he held the dog fast with one hand, and scowled over Christine's note.

"I don't understand," he said, shaking his dark head. "You thought the part about Holly Holliday was about you? How could you?"

"The last page, Zack, look at the last page," she said, pointing a mittened hand at the manuscript. He flipped through it, found the page and read it. A bitter smile quirked on his lips. He shook his head again. "You thought—of course, you thought..." he said. "No wonder. I never even saw..."

He looked down at her sympathetically. "No wonder you were so nasty, you little vixen. He waved the pages above his head. Jana turned her face and saw Christine, still parked by the curb, watching them. "Go to war, blondie! Tell them to can the Holly Holliday chapter. It's caused me enough grief!"

Christine shot him an almost military salute, then turned the key in the ignition.

Zack flung the papers into the air and let go of Sasha's collar. He swept Jana into his arms with such force she lost her breath. She was crushed against his broad chest. He lowered his face and took possession of her lips in a kiss of such dizzying intensity that she had to wind her arms tightly around his neck just to support herself. She heard Christine's car pull away and Sasha leaping through the snow.

He drew his face away and stared down at her.

"You've got snow in your mustache," she said, looking up into the golden eyes, feeling herself drowning in their depths.

"Then melt it off," he murmured, taking her lips beneath his own again. The rightness of it, the joy of it, made her body sing against his. To be in those powerful arms again was like a homecoming, the end of a long and arduously lonely journey.

Sasha sprang against them, knocking Zack off balance. Laughing, he pulled Jana down beside him in the drift, pinning her against him.

"Now I've got more snow to melt," he said. Her cap had come off, and he put his hand in her curls and brought her face to his. Again she felt herself go nearly faint with happiness and desire. He kissed her until Sasha's tugging at his sleeve made him draw away. Then Sasha delivered a kiss of her own, full on Zack's face.

"Ugh!" he laughed. "Go away! I'm going to have to teach you, Sasha, that some moments are sacred. Take a walk. Chase a rabbit. Go build a snowman."

But Sasha only redoubled her affectionate assault, until all three of them were covered with snow and Jana was helpless with laughter. At last the dog bounded away, begging to be chased. Zack ignored her and turned to Jana, brushing the snow from her face. "Sasha hates to be left out," he said. "I'm afraid she'll insist on being a bridesmaid. Or do you object to bridesmaids with long bushy tails and crazed eyes?"

"Is that a proposal?" she asked, raising her hand to his cheek.

"It's the best I can do. I'm new at this." His face was suddenly serious. "You don't know what you put me though this last week, my girl. You were smart to stay at Nell's. For the first two days I had visions of happily strangling you. I couldn't write. I couldn't sleep. I felt like packing it in and taking the first plane out of here just so I wouldn't have to think about you so much."

"You've got to stick around," she said, losing herself in his eyes again. "You've got a great book to write."

He cocked an eyebrow sarcastically. "I thought I couldn't write, in your opinion. I thought I was a hack, then, now and forevermore. And how do you know I'm going to write a great book?"

"Christine said you were writing on Lincoln. And it'll be a great book because you're a great writer."

"Wait," he said, suddenly pulling on his ear and scowling. "Am I going deaf? Do my ears deceive me? You actually said something nice about my writing?"

"I had to work very hard not to like your books, Zack. I was so sure you were up to something that I forced myself not to like them. They're good books. Even the two the critics didn't like. Critics are wrong sometimes. I'm sure you can do it."

"Mmm," he said. "Sweet words. Sweet mouth."

He bent and kissed her, a long, lingering kiss that hinted of delights yet untasted, to be discovered slowly and with sensuous pleasure.

He left her breathless. "Zack," she managed to say, "we ought to get out of the snow. We'll freeze."

"Us?" he said with absolute confidence. "Never,"

# Coming Next Month in Harlequin Romances!

**2731   TEARS OF GOLD   Helen Conrad**
The mystery man found panning for gold on a young woman's
California estate sparks her imagination—especially when she learns
he's bought her family home!

**2732   LORD OF THE AIR   Carol Gregor**
There's turbulence ahead when the owner of a flying school wants
to build a runway on his neighbor's land. He disturbs her privacy,
not to mention her peace of mind....

**2733   SPRING AT SEVENOAKS   Miriam MacGregor**
A young Englishwoman's visit to a New Zealand sheep station
arouses the owner's suspicions. No woman could be counted on to
live in such isolation! Why should she be any different?

**2734   WEDNESDAY'S CHILD   Leigh Michaels**
Is it generosity that prompts a man to offer his estranged wife money
for their son's medical expenses? Or is it a bid to get her under his
thumb again?

**2735   WHERE THE GODS DWELL   Celia Scott**
A fashion photographer abandons her glamorous career for an
archaeological dig in Crete. But she has second thoughts when she
falls in love...and clashes with old-world Greece.

**2736   WILDERNESS BRIDE   Gwen Westwood**
Concern brings an estranged wife to her husband's side on an
African wilderness reserve when blindness threatens him. But he
insists on reconquering the wilderness...and her!

# Readers rave about Harlequin American Romance!

"...the best series of modern romances I have read...great, exciting, stupendous, wonderful."
— S.E.,* Coweta, Oklahoma

"...they are absolutely fantastic...going to be a smash hit and hard to keep on the bookshelves."
— P.D., Easton, Pennsylvania

"The American line is great. I've enjoyed every one I've read so far."
— W.M.K., Lansing, Illinois

"...the best stories I have read in a long time."
— R.H., Northport, New York

*Names available on request.

*You're invited to accept 4 books and a surprise gift Free!*

# Acceptance Card

**Mail to: Harlequin Reader Service®**

In the U.S.
2504 West Southern Ave.
Tempe, AZ 85282

In Canada
P.O. Box 2800, Postal Station A
5170 Yonge Street
Willowdale, Ontario M2N 6J3

**YES!** Please send me 4 free Harlequin American Romance®
novels and my free surprise gift. Then send me 4 brand new novels
as they come off the presses. Bill me at the low price of $2.25 each
—an 11% saving off the retail price. There are no shipping, handling
or other hidden costs. There is no minimum number of books I
must purchase. I can always return a shipment and cancel at any
time. Even if I never buy another book from Harlequin, the 4 free
novels and the surprise gift are mine to keep forever.

154 BPA-BPGE

Name                                (PLEASE PRINT)

Address                                                    Apt. No.

City                        State/Prov.            Zip/Postal Code

This offer is limited to one order per household and not valid to present
subscribers. Price is subject to change.          ACAR-SUB-1

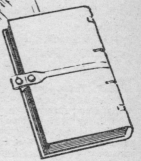

# Take 4 books & a surprise gift FREE

---

## SPECIAL LIMITED-TIME OFFER

Mail to **Harlequin Reader Service®**

| In the U.S. | In Canada |
|---|---|
| 2504 West Southern Ave. | P.O. Box 2800, Station "A" |
| Tempe, AZ 85282 | 5170 Yonge Street |
| | Willowdale, Ontario M2N 6J3 |

**YES!** Please send me 4 free Harlequin Romance® novels and my free surprise gift. Then send me 6 brand-new novels every month as they come off the presses. Bill me at the low price of $1.65 each ($1.75 in Canada)—a 11% saving off the retail price. There are no shipping, handling or other hidden costs. There is no minimum number of books I must purchase. I can always return a shipment and cancel at any time. Even if I never buy another book from Harlequin, the 4 free novels and the surprise gift are mine to keep forever.

---

Name _____ (PLEASE PRINT)

---

Address _____ Apt. No. _____

---

City _____ State/Prov. _____ Zip/Postal Code _____

This offer is limited to one order per household and not valid to present subscribers. Price is subject to change.                    DOR–SUB–1